STEALING LOVE

I0685761

BY
WILLIAM SPEIR

Progressive
RISING PHOENIX PRESS ®

Text Copyright © 2023 William Speir

All rights reserved.
Published 2023 by Progressive Rising Phoenix Press, LLC
www.progressiverisingphoenix.com

ISBN: 978-1-958640-41-8

Printed in the U.S.A.
1st Printing

Cover Photograph: "Beautiful Elegant Couple In Front Of The Eiffel Tower" by Ollyy, ShutterStock Photo ID: 107172497, used under license from ShutterStock.com.
.

Interior Illustration: "Paris France City Skyline Vector Silhouette Illustration" by YurkaImmortal, ShutterStock Photo ID: 153626633, used under license from ShutterStock.com.

Book and Cover design by William Speir
Visit: http://www.williamspeir.com

To my Bonnie Lass, the love of my life, my best friend, and my partner through all the seasons of our lives. Here's to the next twenty-five years, Sweetheart!

PROLOGUE

The phone rang in the home office of Nicolau De la Riva's villa in the *Sarrià-Sant Gervasi* district of Barcelona, Spain. It was early December, and there was a slight chill throughout the villa.

"Hello?" He sounded annoyed at the interruption from the unknown caller.

"Señor De la Riva?" the woman's voice asked.

"Yes. What do you want?" he demanded, guessing from the accent that the woman was North American.

"I'm calling in regards to an art object you recently acquired."

Growing even more annoyed, he grumbled, "And which piece is that? I procure new artwork all the time."

"This is a unique piece that you had to obtain very… shall we say, carefully and dangerously? It's a jeweled gold and jade Madonna, which belonged to the Kang family in Prague until you… acquired the piece for yourself."

"I don't know what you're talking about."

De la Riva was about to slam down the phone, when the woman's voice said, "You most certainly do, Señor De la Riva. Surely you didn't think you were the only party interested in the piece, did you? I can assure you that you weren't. But more than that, I have an offer from the rightful owner, Mr. Kang."

De la Riva hesitated. Then he said, "I still don't know what you're talking about, but if I did, what kind of offer is Mr. Kang willing to make?"

"Mr. Kang is willing to let you keep the item in question, provided you're willing to compensate him for his loss. In return, he will provide a properly-binding bill of sale, allowing you legal ownership of the piece."

"And why should I compensate Mr. Kang for something that his insurance company has undoubtedly already compensated him for? Assuming that I was in possession of the item in question, which I'm not."

"You are mistaken, Señor De la Riva," the woman said. "The Kang family is bankrupt. There was no insurance on the item. He was in the process of selling it to raise the funds necessary to satisfy his creditors. As a result of your acquisition, and the manner of it, the Kang family is ruined. They lost their business, their home, and everything else they owned. The children are now wards of the state, and Mr. Kang and his wife are living in a shelter, destitute. All he wants is a reasonable sum to allow him to reunite his family and live a decent life until he gets back on his feet. Surely not an unreasonable request?"

De la Riva snorted. "Mr. Kang's problems are not my problems. But for the sake of curiosity what does Mr. Kang consider to be a reasonable sum?"

The woman quoted a figure.

"Out of the question," De la Riva stated. "Even if I did possess the item, which I don't, I would never pay that sum for something already in my possession."

"I'll give you twenty-four hours to change your mind, Señor De la Riva," the woman said.

"I don't need twenty-four hours," De la Riva retorted. "My final answer is no. Now, good-bye." He slammed the phone back on its receiver, ending the call.

Amelia "Aimee" Kim stared at her phone. Then she called her business partner.

"Hello?"

"It's me," Aimee said.

"Let me guess," her business partner said. "He refused Kang's offer."

"He did," Aimee confirmed. "You're on for tonight."

"I'll meet you at the pre-arranged location at midnight."

"I'll be there," Aimee promised. Then she added, "One of these days, we're going to have to talk about all these *pro bono* cases you take on."

Her business partner laughed. "We make enough from the insurance companies and the clients willing to pay our fees to allow us a few charity cases. Besides, I was already in Barcelona, so there are no additional expenses being incurred. I'll recover the Madonna tonight, and tomorrow night I'll visit Señor Lovato and recover the chalice stolen from the *Catedral de Sevilla* in Seville. The good people of Barcelona will never remember the nights that *Le Chat Rusé* visited their fair city, but two possessors of illegally obtained art will never forget."

"You're a cunning cat, all right," Aimee said, referring to her business partner's nickname, which translated to "The Cunning Cat" in English. "But if you keep taking chances like this, you're going to run out of lives."

"I know what I'm doing," her business partner said. "Is the next assignment the same one we discussed?"

"Yes, your train reservations are booked, and you've already been checked-in at your hotel. The keys are at the front desk, and your equipment is in the room waiting for you. I'll upload the prey's particulars after you recover the chalice."

"Perfect. Well, I'd better prepare for tonight's caper. See you at midnight."

"I'll be there," Aimee confirmed. She ended the call.

The next morning, Señor De la Riva walked through his villa's personal art gallery. As he approached the Plexiglas display case in the middle of the room, he discovered that the cover was on the floor, and the Madonna was missing. In its place was a white card with the image of a cat picking its teeth along the left border. The words on the card read: *Le Chat Rusé sends greetings.*

De la Riva stared at the card, enraged, knowing that this was a crime that could never be reported to the police.

The following morning, Señor Lovato found a similar card resting on the pedestal where the stolen gold chalice once stood. As he crumpled the card in his clenched fist, he swore, knowing there was nothing he could do to recover what he had stolen in the first place.

Aimee's business partner, the thief known as *Le Chat Rusé,* sat in first-class on the high-speed train, reading the electronic edition of one of the major Barcelona newspapers. There was no mention of any art thefts in the paper.

Aimee had returned the chalice to the *Catedral de Sevilla* that morning, and she would take the Madonna to Mr. Kang in Prague that evening. All-in-all, it had been a good three weeks in Barcelona.

The thief smiled, closed the newspaper app on the tablet, and opened the file with the particulars about the next caper. The item to be recovered was known as "The Van der Waal Peacock" created by artist Horst Van der Waal, who fashioned amazing works of art out of gold and jewels.

The sculpture is solid gold, covered in platinum crystals, diamonds, sapphires, rubies, pearls, and other precious and semi-precious stones. It stands 18-inches tall, is amazingly detailed—particularly the feathers—and weighs nearly 30 pounds. Estimated worth is 30 million euros. We get 10% of its insured value from the insurance company, which works out to three million euros, plus expenses.

The thief then reviewed the details about the target. *This job might take considerably longer than Barcelona did. The prey is clever. He not only has state-of-the-art security, but he also has security guards at both residences. Even after I find out in which of the residences he has the item hidden, I have to figure out how to get in, steal the item, and get back out alive with the item in my possession. This is going to take research, planning, and a great deal of luck. I hate this kind of assignment.*

The thief shut down the tablet and put it in the briefcase on the floor. Watching the sunset as the countryside flew past the train windows, the thief thought about the assignment and how best to start.

CHAPTER 1

J osh MacGregor sat on the train from Barcelona to Paris, trying to see the French countryside outside his window. *The whole reason I took the train was to see the sights, but it's already dark outside, and we still have hours to go before we reach Paris.*

The previous day, December 10th, Josh was in Madrid, completing an assignment for one of his clients. He wanted to take the train to Paris, but there were no direct trains from Madrid. Looking at the various options, he decided to take the 10:00 AM train from Madrid to Barcelona—a city he had recently visited—and catch the high-speed train from there.

The three-hour train ride from Madrid's Atocka Station arrived at Barcelona's Sants Station on time. Because he was traveling first class, he was allowed to spend the ninety-minute layover in the Sala Club First Class Lounge. When the hostess called his train, he gathered his canvas briefcase, garment bag, and oversized roller bag. He exited the Lounge and headed for the escalators that went down to the departure platforms. After he presented his bags for x-ray screening, he took the escalator down to Platform 4 to board the train to Paris.

When he reached his assigned train car, he climbed the stairs to the upper floor, stowed his garment and roller bags on the luggage rack, and found his seat. He placed the briefcase on the floor behind his legs, grabbed his phone, and returned a couple of phone calls while the other first-class passengers found their seats. He had just put his phone away and retrieved the tablet from his briefcase when he saw a tall, attractive woman take the seat across the aisle from him.

What he immediately noticed about her was her steel gray eyes, which gave her a sultry gaze. Her long hair was brunette, but there were auburn streaks throughout that caught the light from the overhead fixtures. She had an athletic build, and like Josh, she was dressed casually for weekend travel, wearing jeans, riding boots, a deep red sweater, and a black jacket.

He watched her place a soft-sided briefcase—similar to his own—on the floor and remove a tablet. As he glanced at the screen, he saw that she was reading the English edition of the local newspaper. *Must be British or an American*, he concluded.

Josh opened the Spanish edition of one of the Barcelona papers. Even though he was originally from Atlanta, Georgia, his work was in Europe, so he always read the newspapers in the local dialect to keep his language skills sharp. He was fluent in Spanish, French, and Italian, but he wanted to learn Russian and German so he could accept assignments in those countries.

As the train pulled out of the station and headed north, he finished reading the Barcelona paper and then opened the French edition of one of the Paris papers. Seeing nothing of interest, he closed the newspaper apps and opened the file that contained the details of his assignment in Paris.

Raphaël Janvier, owner of The Janvier Group, was a Parisian business tycoon and art collector. His company included seven subsidiaries—most of which had grown through acquisitions that had never been integrated. Reading the biography of his new client, Josh noted that Janvier had an apartment attached to his office in the 38-story tower known as The Carpe Diem on *Place des Corolles* in the part of Paris known as La Defense. Janvier's company occupied floors 27-31. His main residence was a 20 room, 6-bedroom, 7 level mansion in the Porte Dauphine District of Paris, southwest of the Eiffel Tower and the Arc de Triomphe.

Josh glanced at the photos of Janvier's house. *I've heard he throws lavish parties at the mansion. I wonder if I'll be invited to any of them. I'd love to see the interior of both residences.*

After finishing the information Josh's firm had sent him, he turned off the tablet and put it back in his briefcase. Then he looked out the window to watch the scenery. As the train passed through northern Spain, heading for the border, the sun sank lower in the west. By the time they crossed into France, it was hard to see any of the countryside, and soon it was too dark to see anything out the windows at all.

Josh glanced at the woman across the aisle. She had stopped reading her tablet and was staring out the window. *At least she has the sunset through her window.*

He debated whether he should disturb her, but given that they still had four hours to go before reaching Paris, and the first-class car was less than half-full, he decided to take a chance. "Can you see anything out there?" he asked.

She turned and smiled. "No, it's too dark. You?"

"Same," he said, guessing from her accent that she was from somewhere along the east coast of the United States. "I was just about to visit the café-bar in car four and grab something to eat. Care to join me?"

The woman looked at him intently for a moment. Then she smiled again and said, "Sure, why not?"

She stood and held out her hand. "I'm Erica. Erica Longwood"

Josh shook her hand. "Josh MacGregor."

They went to the lower level of their train car and walked to car four. After climbing the stairs to the upper level, where the café-bar was located, they grabbed an empty table. The printed menus listed a large assortment of beverages, sandwiches, hot dishes, and snacks.

After they had made their selection, Josh placed their order at the bar. When he returned to the table with their beverages, he sat and said, "So, Erica, I'm guessing from your accent that you're from somewhere in the mid-Atlantic part of the States."

"Correct," she said pleasantly. "Northern Virginia. You?"

"Georgia, but I haven't been back in years. I spend my time in Europe these days."

"Doing what?" she asked.

"I'm a business strategy consultant. I just finished an assignment in Madrid, and I start a new one tomorrow in Paris. The client is a company that has grown through a number of acquisitions, but they've never integrated the pieces together into a company with a single way of working. That's where I come in. My job is to turn the client's operations into a single company so they can grow more without flying apart at the seams."

"Do you enjoy that work?" Erica asked.

"I love it," Josh answered. "I like helping people do their best work." He took a drink. "What about you? What takes you to Paris?"

"I'm an interior designer," Erica replied.

"Commercial or private facilities?" Josh asked.

"Both," she said. "I've designed homes, hotels, office buildings… anywhere that people live or work. I finished an assignment with two homes in Spain, met with a friend from college while I was in Barcelona, and now I'm heading for Paris to see if I can land a new client there. I'm supposed to be bringing in new business if I want a promotion, and Paris seems to be a great market to find potential business."

"Even during the holiday season?" Josh asked.

"It takes a while to land a new client, so I'd rather start in December while clients are finalizing their budgets for next year, rather than wait until January after the budgets are already fixed. That way, the client still has time to allocate the funds needed for my services."

Josh nodded. "Good strategy—"

The server arrived with their club sandwiches and fries.

As they began eating, Josh asked, "How long do you expect to be in Paris?"

Erica shrugged. "It could take until February to land a new client, and then I'll be there for however long the assignment lasts. Could be months. Could be years. What about you? How long are you planning to stay in Paris?"

"Three months minimum. Possibly six, depending on what I find after I start peeling back the layers."

"Do you have a place there?" Erica asked.

"The client has me set up in a hotel near the office. Hôtel Mgallery Nest Paris in the La Defense district. What about you?"

"For now, I'm staying at the Hotel Elysées Ceramic, on *Avenue de Wagram*. If I read the map correctly, it's northeast of the Arc de Triomphe and south of the *Avenue de Ternes/Rue du Faubourg Saint-Honoré*. If I land the client, I'll probably get an apartment close to the worksite for the duration of the assignment."

Josh nodded. "Sounds like we both spend a lot of time in hotels."

"It's the life we chose, right? I live out of a suitcase and eat mostly room service. I sold my place back home years ago, and now I live the nomad life."

"Me, too," Josh admitted. "I put most of my things in storage, and I just travel with enough clothes for ten days."

"How does that work, if you're on assignment for months at a time?" Erica asked.

"Hotel laundries," Josh replied. "And if I need something new, I buy it local. Once you get used to the routine, it's not that hard."

They chatted for a while longer and finished eating, but as the café-bar grew more crowded, they decided to head back to their seats. When they reached their car and headed up the stairs, Josh said, "Is there any chance you'd like to get together while we're in Paris? With the holidays coming up, it's too beautiful a city to spend Christmas and New Year's alone."

Erica didn't say anything until they had reached their seats. Then she replied, "I don't normally mix business with pleasure—especially since I'm here to generate new business—but you make an interesting point. Let me see how work is going, and I'll call you. Do you have a card with your phone number?"

Josh nodded and procured a card from his briefcase. Erica handed him one of her cards as well.

Erica looked at Josh's card. *MacGregor has a rogue-ish feel to it. I like that.* She put the card in her shirt pocket. She had no intention of calling him. When she said she didn't normally mix business and pleasure, she should have said that she *never* mixed business and pleasure. It was one of her hard and fast rules. The endless travel made relationships impractical, if not impossible. She devoted 100% of her effort to her business. Men were a distraction that she felt she didn't need. She planned to toss his card into the first trash can she passed by. But for some reason, she found herself not wanting to get rid of his number.

She glanced over at Josh. *There's something about him. He's different. Yes, we're both from southern states, but there's something else that I can't put my finger on. I'm comfortable with him, and that's a rare thing. I had forgotten what that feels like.*

She tried to remember the last real relationship she had been in, and she realized it was her senior year of college. *Fourteen years, and it ended badly. Ha! Badly is an understatement. It devastated me, and it screwed up my dating life ever since. I haven't even had a decent one-night-stand in the last six years at least.* She glanced at Josh again. *He's certainly handsome. I like his blue eyes, light brown hair, and strong chin. He's tall, but not too tall.* She tried to stop thinking about him, but she couldn't. *And he's right. Paris over the holidays is a magical place. And clients don't work on Christmas or New Year's. Maybe I will spend some time with him over the holidays. Worst case, I'm not alone on Christmas for once. Best case, I have some fun for a change before we both leave for our next assignments. What's the harm in that? We're both adults, we're both single, and we're both in Paris. I should be able to handle this and still get my work done.*

A few minutes before 9:30 PM, the train pulled into Paris Gare De Lyon Station on *Pl. Louis-Armand*, arriving in Hall 1 on the ground level. When the train slowed to a stop, Josh stood and helped Erica to her feet. He retrieved his garment bag and roller bag, and he handed Erica her roller bag. Then they disembarked the train.

As they headed for the ground transportation, Josh asked, "Would you like to get a late supper before heading to your hotel?"

Erica hesitated, but then she said. "You and I both start our new assignments in the morning. Probably best that we call it a night. I'd suggest sharing a cab, but we're heading in separate directions."

"Then this is where we part company," Josh said, disappointed.

"For now," Erica said quickly.

Josh nodded.

As they reached the queue for cabs, they stood in silence, both wondering if they'd actually see each other again. When it was Erica's turn for a cab, Josh said, "I enjoyed our time together on the train."

"So did I," Erica said as she handed her bag to the driver. "I look forward to seeing you again, Josh."

"I do, too, Erica."

She smiled at him and got into her cab. As it disappeared into the night, Josh couldn't stop thinking about her. *She is the most beautiful woman I've ever met. I hope this wasn't a one-time-only meeting... but it probably was.*

The next cab pulled up, and Josh helped the driver put the bags into the trunk. Josh then climbed into the back seat and gave the driver the address of his hotel.

CHAPTER 2

osh woke up the next morning just before his alarm went off. He rose quickly, showered, and dressed in his best suit. This was his first day at The Janvier Group, and he wanted to make a good impression. His first meeting of the day was with Raphaël Janvier himself, and this meeting would set the tone for the rest of the assignment.

He put on his overcoat, walked down the hotel hallway, and rode the elevator to the ground floor. The Janvier Group had a continuous-running shuttle every morning and afternoon that went between the hotel and the office, since the company used this hotel for its out-of-town employees and contractors. The Hôtel Mgallery Nest Paris boasted a five-star rating, and Josh found it to be quite comfortable. The hotel had definitely been designed with foreign travelers in mind, who were accustomed to larger hotel rooms and finer amenities.

The shuttled had just pulled up to the main lobby doors when Josh emerged from the elevator. He crossed the lobby, exited the hotel, and climbed onboard the shuttle for the eight-minute ride to the office building. Even though the office was close enough to walk to, the traffic made it too dangerous, and the weather made it a chilly twenty-five-minute trek.

When he arrived at the office building, he was directed to

the security office, where his passport was scrutinized, he was photographed, and he received an entry card with his image printed on it that granted him access to the building, the elevators, and the floors that The Janvier Group occupied. The Janvier Group's security would be responsible for handling his access to the offices on floors 27 through 31.

Josh rode up the elevators to the 27th floor. He was met by a stern looking gentleman when the elevator doors opened.

"Josh MacGregor?" the man asked with a German accent.

Josh nodded.

"Excellent. My name is Günter Reinhardt. I'm head of security for The Janvier Group. Follow me, please."

Josh followed the tall, balding man to the Security office just off the main lobby. At first glance, Josh estimated that the man was in his early 50s, but he looked like he could still play rugby with the best players in the world and beat them all. Josh wondered what Reinhardt's tailors charged to craft a suit around his muscular frame.

Reinhardt led Josh into a mid-sized conference room. "Building security has already forwarded your photo and the copy of your passport, so we have them on file," Reinhardt stated. He handed Josh a lanyard, which had "The Janvier Group" stitched across it. Attached was a key card with "TJG" embossed on it. "This key card is your access to our offices on floors 27 through 31. It will give you entry through the main doors, the stairway entrances, and most of the common areas on each of our floors. There are secure sections of our offices that this card will not grant you entry. To gain entry, you must be escorted by someone authorized for those areas. Understand?"

"Yes, sir," Josh acknowledged.

"Good. Keep your building access card on this same lanyard, with your photo facing forward at all times. Otherwise, Security will stop you."

"I understand," Josh said.

Reinhardt smiled for the first time. "Welcome to The Janvier Group, Mr. MacGregor. I'll take you up to Mr. Janvier's office now, since that's one of the areas your key card will not grant you access."

"Thank you."

Josh followed Reinhardt back to the elevators. Once inside, Reinhardt swiped his key card past the card reader and pressed the button for the 31st floor. A moment later, the elevator doors opened. Reinhardt led Josh through three security doors, pointing out which ones Josh's key card would open and which ones it wouldn't.

When they entered Janvier's outer office, Reinhardt said, "I leave you here. If you have any problem accessing the offices, come to the Security office on 27 and someone will help you."

Josh shook his hand and winced at Reinhardt's grip. Then Reinhardt left the office.

Janvier's receptionist stood. "Mr. MacGregor? Mr. Janvier is expecting you. Right this way."

Josh followed her through a large doorway and into the most impressive, grand office he had ever seen. A slim, older man—with salt-and-pepper hair, tanned skin, and tinted glasses—stood up from behind the desk at the far end.

"Mr. MacGregor, welcome to The Janvier Group. I'm Raphaël Janvier. Please be seated."

Josh walked forward and sat in the seat Janvier gestured toward. The office was illuminated by two lamps on Janvier's desk, picture lights over the artwork on the walls, and ambient lighting around the edge of the ceiling. The blinds were closed to block the morning sunlight from shining through the windows, and Josh would later discover that Janvier didn't like open blinds or curtains, regardless of the view.

Janvier took his seat behind the massive live-edged wooden desk. "Tell Mr. Laurent to join us in fifteen minutes," Janvier said to his receptionist.

"Yes, sir," she answered before closing the office door behind her.

Looking at Josh, Janvier said, "Étienne Laurent is my head of Operations, and he will be your principal point-of-contact while you're here. Now, I know you're probably eager to get started, so let me give you an idea of what I'm looking for, and you can tell me how you plan to accomplish what I need done."

Erica rose early, dressed, and had a quick breakfast in the hotel's café. She had been doing a great deal of research on the man she had come to Paris to see, and it was time to determine the best way to approach him.

She drove the car that had been rented for her to the *Porte Dauphine* District in the 16th *Arrondissement* of Paris. At the end of a closed square, filled with impressive side-by-side mansions, sat the private residence of the man she was there to meet. The house was seven levels; a wrought iron gated fence surrounded the front lawn, and large Tuscan Cypress Trees flanked the front porch and steps on both sides, forming a natural windbreak that provided privacy from the neighbors.

She parked the car down the street, where she could observe the house, making notes of everything she saw. She walked around to the entrance of the courtyard shared by the houses on that block, so she could see the house from the rear. After a while, she thought, *There's no way I can approach him here at his home. From what I've read, he leaves for work early and comes home late. If he sees me here, it will have to be on a weekend and only with an appointment. I'd do better meeting with him at his office. But how do I get an appointment to see him at his office? He probably has an army of secretaries and receptionists whose job is to keep people like me from getting in to see him. But… it can't hurt to try.*

She returned to her car, pulled out her phone, and dialed a number. When the call was answered, she said, "Yes, my name is Erica Longwood with Le Luxe Interiors. I'd like to make an appointment with Mr. Janvier."

"May I ask what this is concerning?" the receptionist asked.

"My firm wishes to add The Janvier Group as a client, and I'd like to discuss what we can do for him and his company."

"He's very busy," the receptionist said.

"I only need ten minutes. This is a preliminary conversation only. If the meeting is successful, I'll schedule a follow-up where I can present a full proposal for our services."

There was a long pause. Then the receptionist said, "One moment. I'll transfer you to his private secretary."

"Thank you," Erica said pleasantly. *First hurdle crossed. Now for the second and more difficult one.*

A moment later, another woman answered the phone. "Miss Longwood? This is Jenevieve Blanchard, Mr. Janvier's private secretary. I understand you wish to make an appointment."

"That's right," Erica confirmed.

"And the name of your firm is Le Luxe Interiors?"

"Correct," Erica said.

"Is that an interior design firm?"

"Yes, we design for hotels, offices, and residences."

"And why do you wish to meet with Mr. Janvier?"

"We understand that he is planning an expansion sometime in the next year, and that usually means new office space will be required. We can help locate suitable office space, design the layout, and oversee all of the work required to create the perfect working environment. We can also help any of the relocating staff to find housing, identify any renovations required or desired, and oversee the work to renovate the residences into homes worthy of the new owners and their positions. We have an outstanding track record in our field, and I think we have much to offer Mr. Janvier and his company."

"I see…" Blanchard said. There was a pause. "He's quite busy. I don't think there's any way he'll have time to meet you before the first of the year."

"I can meet him anytime day or night," Erica said quickly, "and anywhere that is most convenient for him."

"Hmmmm," Blanchard said. "Let me discuss this with him, and I'll let you know what he says. Can you be reached at this number?"

"Yes. Thank you."

"We'll be in touch, Miss Longwood." The call ended.

Erica dialed the number of her business partner. "Getting in through the front door might be difficult," she said when her partner answered the phone.

"Secretary barring the doors?" her partner asked.

"As per usual," Erica confirmed. "I may get in that way, but I'll start cultivating other options, just in case."

"Keep me informed." The call ended.

Erica drove to La Defense and parked close to The Carpe Diem tower. After entering the lobby, she walked around for a while. In one corner of the lobby, there was a display showing the building's construction and some of the architect diagrams. She studied the diagrams for a while, photographed several with her phone, and then left the building.

She purchased a large coffee from one of the vendors on the plaza and watched the building for a while. She was about to return to her car when she saw a familiar face exiting the building. It was Josh, and he was walking with another man that she didn't recognize.

Josh works here? She thought about how he had described his assignment in Paris. *If he's working for Janvier, then he might be my way past Janvier's blockade. It's a good thing I decided not to throw away his card after all. Perhaps I should call him and suggest dinner. If he is working for Janvier, I might be able to convince him to put in a good word for me. And if*

14

not… well, at least I'll have company for dinner.

She walked back to her car and drove to her hotel.

Étienne Laurent has assigned Josh a large office on the 30th floor, where Operations was headquartered, and it was filled with reports, organization charts, and other materials that Josh needed to review before making any recommendations to his client.

At 5:00 PM, Josh decided to head back to his hotel. He put on his overcoat, grabbed his briefcase, and closed the office door behind him. It was self-locking, and his key card had already been programmed to open the door.

As he headed for the elevator, his cell phone rang. "Hello?" he answered.

"Hi, is this… Josh?" a woman's voice asked.

"Yes, it is."

"Hi, Josh, this is Erica… from the train yesterday."

Josh's pulse quickened. "Hi, Erica! I'm glad you called. What can I do for you?"

"Are you free for dinner?"

"I have no plans at the moment," he replied.

"Neither do I," Erica purred. "I don't know what the dining options are around your hotel, but there are over two hundred restaurants in walking distance of mine. Do you mind coming over here?"

"Tell me again where you're staying," Josh said.

"It's the Hotel Elysées Ceramic. The address is 34 *Avenue de Wagram*, 75008. It's northeast of the Arc de Triomphe and south of the *Avenue de Ternes/Rue du Faubourg Saint-Honoré*."

Josh made a mental note of her hotel's address. "I can probably be there in an hour, depending on traffic," he said. "Fancy or casual?"

"How about casual for tonight," Erica suggested.

"Tonight?" Josh asked.

"Well… just in case we decide to have dinner again another night."

Josh chuckled. "Okay. I'm just leaving the office now. It'll take a few minutes to get to my hotel and change, and then I'll catch a cab and head your way. Meet you in your lobby?"

"Call me when you get here," she suggested.

"Will do. See you soon. And thanks again for calling. I'm looking forward to it. Bye."

"Bye."

Josh rode down the crowded elevator with a smile on his face. He took the shuttle back to his hotel, went to his room to change clothes, and was back in the lobby in under ten minutes. He caught a cab, gave the driver Erica's address, and sat back as the cab pulled out into the evening Paris traffic. It was slow going, but Josh finally arrived at Erica's hotel a few minutes after six.

Erica stepped off the elevator into her hotel's lobby and saw Josh walk through the street entrance. He had his phone in his hand, and when he saw her, she waved to him. *I don't want Josh to know that I have a car here in Paris. If he's a gentleman, he'll want to pick me up and drop me off… and if he's not, I don't want him thinking that I can pick him up and drop him off.*

As she walked toward him, she felt a slight fluttering in her stomach. *I hope that's because I'm hungry and not because I'm attracted to him. I don't have time for that kind of complication in my life.*

"I was about to call you," he said when she reached him.

"I figured you were almost here, so I decided to wait for you in the lobby," she explained. "What are you hungry for?"

"What do you recommend?" Josh asked.

16

"There's a great little Italian place around the corner. Want to go there?"

Josh grinned. "I love Italian food."

"Then follow me."

Erica led the way. They exited the hotel, crossed the street, and walked to the corner. The restaurant was that close, and even though it looked busy they were seated immediately.

"Have you eaten here before?" Josh asked, looking at the menu.

"A couple of times," Erica replied. "There are times you just need a pizza, and the pizza here is great."

"Pizza it is!"

They decided what kind of pizza they wanted. The waiter came over to the table, and Erica gestured for Josh to order for the both of them. Josh ordered a large pizza for them to share, and a bottle of the restaurant's house wine with two glasses.

Erica was impressed. *I'll bet the waiter thinks he's a local.* "Your French is quite good," she said aloud after the waiter had left. "I can hold my own in a conversation, but you speak it like it's your native language."

"It took years of practice," Josh conceded. "The trick is the accent. If they think for even a second that you're an American, they're merciless to you from that moment on. It's different outside Paris, but here in the city… it's like they have a moral imperative to be as rude as possible to people from the States."

"That explains a lot," she said.

"How do you mean?" Josh asked.

Erica leaned forward and lowered her voice. "Case in point. Today, I tried to get an appointment with the head of a big company that I want to land as a new client. I got past the receptionist, but the guy's private secretary wouldn't budge. Oh, she said she'd talk to him and call me back, but I doubt I'll hear from her again. I had to call my business partner to tell her that I failed, and it sucked. Most of my year-end bonuses are linked to

17

landing Janvier as a client."

Josh perked up at the name Erica mentioned. "Janvier? You mean Raphaël Janvier? The head of The Janvier Group?"

Erica nodded. "Yeah, he has an office in The Carpe Diem Tower. I took a cab over there today to see about getting an appointment, but it was no go. Why?"

"Because he's my new client," Josh said. "I started work there today."

Erica laughed. "That's a hell-of-a-thing! Who knew? You never mentioned that on the train."

"And you didn't mention him either," Josh said. "So, if you can't get an appointment to see him, how are you going to pitch him your services?"

"No clue. There has to be a way, but I haven't thought of it yet. I don't want to stalk him… you know, confront him in front of his house or at the store or on a sidewalk. But I need to get an appointment to see him somehow."

The waiter brought the wine to the table, opened the bottle, and left them alone.

Erica's phone went off. She looked at the number and pressed the button to ignore the call.

"Do you need to answer that?" Josh asked.

Erica shook her head. "No, it's just my business partner wanting to know if I've had any bright ideas. I'll call her back when I think of something."

Josh poured the wine. He raised his glass and said, "Here's to bright ideas."

Erica smiled and raised her glass. "To bright ideas. May they come soon."

They drank their wine and chatted for a while. Erica noticed Josh staring at her, so she asked, "What are you looking at?"

"Your eyes," he confessed, blushing slightly. "I've never seen steel-gray eyes before. I can't stop looking at them. Sorry if it seems weird."

Erica laughed. "It's not the first time I've had someone stare at my eyes, but you're the first one who's blushed when he got caught. That makes it kind of charming, rather than weird." *God, did I really just say that? What's wrong with me? I need him to get to Janvier, but I don't need to act like some love-sick school girl to pull that off. If I don't get it together, I'm going to wind up in bed with him, and that's something I really don't need. Geez, now I'm thinking about sleeping with him. What's gotten into me?*

The pizza arrived, and Erica was relieved to have something else to think about.

"So, what's the office space like at The Janvier Group?" she asked after finishing her first slice of pizza.

"Janvier has the 27th through the 31st floors," Josh replied. "I'm on the 30th floor where Operations is located, and the space is utilitarian. Not much effort was taken to create any sort of environment. The 27th floor, where security and the main reception area are located is nice, and the conference rooms and the open spaces seem to have been designed to impress without being 'over the top.' The 31st floor, where the executive suites are located, is beautiful. Teak wood walls, live edge wooden tops for the desks and conference tables, Persian rugs, and lots of artwork all around. There's no theme *per se*, but it's obvious that it was expensively decorated. I don't know about the other floors. I've heard that Janvier has an apartment attached to his office, but I didn't get to see it. I did overhear a lot of gossip today about what goes on in that apartment after hours with someone named... Jenevieve. It's amazing what you can learn when your office is next to the break room."

Erica snorted. "Jenevieve Blanchard? She's Janvier's private secretary. She's the one who wouldn't schedule an appointment for me."

Erica picked up another slice. *Keep it casual. Don't let him know why you're asking specific questions.* "I understand he has quite an extensive art collection. Did you happen to see any display cases? What I mean is: Is the art just on the walls, or are there statues or figurines? I'm trying to get a feel for Janvier's taste in art and decorating. It could help with my pitch, if I ever get to make it."

Josh nodded. "I understand. And no, I didn't see any display cases or freestanding art. It all appeared to be paintings and murals. I don't know about the apartment."

Erica ate her slice of pizza. Josh poured the rest of the wine into their glasses.

"Shall I order another bottle?" he asked.

"Please do," Erica replied with a smile.

Josh gestured for the waiter, and when he arrived, Josh ordered the wine. The waiter returned with the bottle a minute later, opened it, and left them alone again.

"Good service here," Josh commented. "And great food. This was a good suggestion you had."

"Thanks. I like it here. It reminds me of being back in the States. The local pizzerias were my hangouts all through high school and college."

"I just realized I don't know where you went to college or where you grew up," Josh said.

"I got my B.S. from Marymount University in Arlington, Virginia," Erica replied. "I have a double-major in Interior Design and Art History. As for where I grew up... mostly in Northern Virginia outside of D.C. My parents were athletes, so I spent my summers learning gymnastics, track, swimming, and rock climbing. That area is beautiful and a great place to grow up. What about you?"

"I have a B.A. with a double-major in Business and Management Sciences from Emory University in Atlanta, where I grew up. I also have an MBA from Johns Hopkins."

"Wow, I guess that really prepared you for what you're doing now," Erica commented.

Josh nodded. "The sad part is: I used to be a swimmer and a runner, but who has time for that anymore? Most of my running is through airports and train stations now, and I can't remember the last time I went for a swim. It's crazy… I get to work in the most beautiful cities in the world, and the only parts of them I get to see are between the airport and my hotel, and between the hotel and the client's offices."

"That's too bad," Erica sympathized. "When I get to a new city for work, I make certain that I take the time to experience all that it has to offer. I don't want to miss a thing, in case I never get back there again."

"I wish I could do that," Josh lamented. "I'm well-travelled, but all of my memories are of my work, not where I did the work. Thanks to you, I've already seen more of Paris than I did of Madrid, and I've only been here for a day."

Erica smiled. "Well, I'm glad I was able to help you experience a sample of what Paris has to offer." *I can't ask him to help me. It has to be his idea. If I'm going to get him to want to help me meet with Janvier, I'd better suggest something he can't resist.* "You know, the holidays in Paris are something not to be missed. How about this? Let me be your guide. Put yourself in my hands, and I'll show you what it's like being in Paris at Christmas and New Year's. Even The Janvier Group has to take time off over the holidays, right? Rather than spend that time working in your hotel out there in La Defense, let's spend it immersing ourselves in this fantastic city. What do you say?"

"That's a hard offer to say 'no' to," Josh commented. He hesitated, then he said, "Okay. Let's do it. I'd like to be able to say that I spent quality time with a beautiful woman in one European city before I get recalled to the States."

Erica laughed. She raised her glass and said, "To the best Paris experience you could possibly imagine."

Josh walked Erica back to her hotel. When they reached the lobby, she said, "I'd love for the evening to continue, but we both have to work tomorrow. And I have a rule about what I do and don't do on first dates."

"Second dates," Josh corrected her.

She cocked her head to one side. "What do you mean, 'second date'?"

"When we went to the café-bar on the train." Josh said. "That was our first date."

Erica stared at him for a moment, and then she laughed. "You're right. This *is* the second date. Sadly, I have rules about those, too."

"I understand." Josh gave her a kiss on the cheek. "Thanks for tonight. I look forward to the next time we get together."

"Let's talk later in the week," Erica said. "Maybe we can get together Wednesday or Thursday, if our schedules permit."

Josh nodded. "Give me a call."

"I will. Good night."

"Good night, Erica."

Josh walked outside and hailed a cab back to his hotel.

Erica walked to the elevator and pressed the button. She pulled out her phone and saw that she had five missed calls. *I'll call her when I get upstairs.*

Raphaël Janvier walked through the west gallery on the sixth floor of his Paris mansion, on the way to his home office at the far end of the gallery. All around him were priceless pieces of artwork that he had acquired through less than legal means. He stopped when he reached the freestanding display case containing his newest acquisition.

The jewel-encrusted peacock was magnificent, even though

it was only eighteen inches tall. The core was solid gold, adorned with diamonds, sapphires, rubies, pearls, a variety of semi-precious stones, and platinum crystals. The piece was worth twenty-five million euros in gold and jewels alone, but as an original work of art, it was worth closer to thirty million.

Janvier smiled as he looked at it. His men had stolen the object from the collector who had originally commissioned the piece for his wife. Now, it belonged to Janvier for his own pleasure.

He glanced up at the blank wall between the two windows overlooking the front of the house. Every time he saw the empty space, it filled him with irritation. *When is that hole going to be filled? My men know where the piece resides, and it's time to liberate it and bring it here. The collector who possesses it now has had it long enough. It's my turn. Besides, he had it stolen for his own enjoyment, so it's not like he can report the theft, and as long as he never finds out that I have it, there's nothing he can do about it, is there?*

Janvier continued to his office. Once seated behind his desk, he called the security room on the first floor.

"Yes, sir?" the guard answered the call.

"Tell Marco and his crew that I want to see them immediately."

"Yes, sir."

Thirty minutes later, five men entered Janvier's office. These men, like the security guards protecting the house, were ex-mercenaries who gave the impression of being dangerous thugs rather than private security operatives. The men were huge, muscle-bound brutes who cared little for the law—only in getting the job done for Janvier. In that regard, they were loyal to a fault, for which Janvier paid them handsomely.

"You wanted to see us, Boss?" Marco asked.

"Yes," Janvier replied smoothly. "Where are we on acquiring my Rembrandt?"

"With your approval, we'll procure it this weekend."

"You have my approval," Janvier said.

"And if there is any… resistance?" Marco asked.

"No witnesses, no interference," Janvier said. "I don't want anyone knowing that you took it or that I have it. Understood?"

"Understood, Boss."

"Thank you, Marco. Let me know when you have my painting."

"And what about the frame?" Marco asked.

"If you can remove it with the frame, do so. If the frame turns out to be a hindrance, leave it behind, but don't let the canvas or the painting be damaged in any way. I don't pay for damaged goods, nor do I employ those who damage my property during its acquisition. *Capiche*?"

"Yes, sir."

Aimee Kim was frustrated. She had been trying to reach *Le Chat Rusé* for hours, but her calls kept going to voice mail. She decided to try one more time that night. She dialed the number and waited.

"Hello?"

"Where have you been?" Aimee demanded. "I've been trying to reach you all evening."

"I know. Sorry about that. I was… busy."

"What do you mean you were busy? Do you have what the client wanted recovered yet?"

"Of course not. I told you before that this job was going to take time."

"Do you have a game plan worked out yet?"

"Yes. Since I can't get an appointment to meet with the target, I'll see if I can make appointments with the companies on the floors above and the floors below his offices. There are two auxiliary central air and maintenance shafts that run from basement to roof. I can use that to enter the secure parts of the target's offices, if I can get access to the shaft."

"How do you know about the shafts?" Aimee asked.

"There's a blueprint display in the building lobby. It showed a cut-away of the building. One shaft is with the elevators in the center of the building, and one is for the water and plumbing halfway between the main shaft and the outer walls. That shaft should allow me to bypass most of the security doors, since those should be closer to the elevators."

"Nice." Aimee wrote herself a note. "I'll find out the companies on those floors and who the points of contact are. Have you thought about trying to infiltrate using the cleaning crew?"

"Yes, but you know the risks of that. If someone notices that I'm missing, it'll raise suspicions. It's best that I don't do my thing with potential witnesses around."

"Understood," Aimee conceded. "What else? What about the private residence?"

"That's going to prove trickier, but I think the fronts of the residences on that block are all façades. I looked at the aerial photos online, and if I can gain access to one of the houses on either side of the target's, I might be able to access his residence from the roof. What makes this trickier is this: First, I have to gain access to one of the other residences in order to access the roof; second, I need to study the floorplans and the security systems of the target's residence so I know where and how to penetrate. That means not only signing up one of his neighbors as a client, but it also means finding the contractor who undoubtedly renovated the residence when he bought it, obtaining the updated floorplans, finding the company that installed and monitors the security system, and obtaining the security schematics. Without all that, I don't have a prayer of getting in and back out safely, not to mention recovering the client's property. But even with all that information, there's another wrinkle at the main residence."

"What's that?" Aimee asked.

"The security guards on site. At one point, I saw a van arrive, dropping off the next shift of guards and picking up the previous shift. Looking at them, I could tell in an instant that they were no ordinary guards from a normal security company. These were well-armed and well-trained thugs. From what I observed, they're undoubtedly part of his illegal businesses, leading me to believe that he runs his criminal empire from the house and his legitimate empire from the offices in La Defense. I counted six guards arriving and leaving, and if they're on duty around the clock, it's going to complicate my entrance and exit strategies."

"Understood. You'll need to factor in their presence when you decide how best to approach the house." Amine wrote down additional notes. "I'll try to find out who the renovation contractor was and who installed the security system... and the interior designer, if you think that'll help. I'll leave the neighbors to you. Is it necessary to access the roofs via one of the other residences?"

"I could scale the outer wall or one of the façades, but I'd be in plain view of more than a dozen security cameras. I'd have the same problem scaling one of the walls of the inner courtyard."

"You checked it out?"

"Yes. Almost every house has a security camera in the courtyard, as well as in the front. I'd be seen. I also saw floodlights in the courtyard, making a night climb just as risky."

"Damn," Aimee swore. "Sounds like you'll either have to gain entrance to a neighbor's house to get to the roof, or you'll have to find a way in through the front door."

"That would be a neat trick."

"I know," Aimee agreed. "Anything else I should know?"

"There was an... unexpected development today that I guess I should mention."

"What?" Aimee demanded.

"I told you that I haven't made any progress getting into the target's office residence. That may have changed tonight."

"How?"

"I met someone named Josh MacGregor who works for the target. I might be able to use him as my entrée to one or both of the target's residences. We had dinner tonight."

Aimee sat speechless. "Erica, have you lost your mind? You know you have rules about mixing business with pleasure, not to mention your rules about dating."

"We're not dating," Erica stated. "He's someone I can leverage to find the object I'm supposed to recover. Nothing more. He's a consultant working for The Janvier Group. I might be able to use him to get past the receptionists and private secretaries. If it works, it was worth it. And besides, what's the harm in having dinner with someone if it's work-related? I haven't broken any of my rules, and I don't plan to. But if he can open doors for me, it could shave weeks off this caper and help keep the client's fees for my expenses down. It's a win-win, Aimee, and you know it. Besides, it's not the first time I've used an insider to open doors that I couldn't open myself."

"Yes, and remember how it turned out the last time?"

"How could I forget?" Erica snapped. "But I learned my lesson, and I'm not going to do that again. He's a means to an end, and that's all. Don't worry."

"It's my job to worry," Aimee said. "I have a business to run. Look, you're one of my oldest and dearest friends. We've known each other since college. But you take too many risks, and this one could get you killed, if you're not careful. But you're going to do things your way, so all I'll say is: Be careful."

"I will," Erica promised. "Talk soon."

"Erica..." Aimee's voice was firm. "Don't sleep with him."

"I swear I won't, okay? Bye."

Aimee ended the call. She stared at the phone for a minute, shaking her head. *I hope she knows what she's doing. This adds unnecessary risk, and she knows it. Well, as long as she doesn't fall for the guy, we might get through this assignment safely and successfully. Just in case, running a background check on this Josh guy couldn't hurt.*

Erica put her phone down and stared at the ceiling. *I don't like lying to Aimee. She's like family. And she's right. This isn't the best idea I could have, but if it works, it'll be worth it. I just can't let myself get distracted. I have a job to do, and Josh is just a way to get that job done.*

Erica shook her head. *And there I go… I'm either lying to myself or trying to convince myself. Honestly, he's cute, and I like him. Yes, I'm using him, and if I'm not careful, or if I were in any other line of work, I could fall for him easily. I can't deny that I'm attracted to him. Frankly, I wouldn't mind sleeping with him—just to remember what it feels like to be with someone. But I have a job to do and can't let things get out of hand with Josh. I don't want to hurt him, I don't want to get hurt, and I don't want to lose focus. I'll tease and string him along until he gives me something I can use to finish the caper, and then I'll disappear, and he'll be left wondering what happened. He'll learn a valuable lesson, and I'll be off on the next assignment… and that will be that.*

Erica stood and started getting ready for bed. *And there I go, trying to convince myself again…*

CHAPTER 3

Wednesday, December 14, Erica called Josh at noon.

"Are you free for dinner tonight?" she asked.

"I have a meeting that won't end until six, so I can be at your hotel between seven and seven-thirty," he responded. "Is that okay with you?"

"That's perfect," Erica replied. "Wear whatever you're wearing now. This will be a bit fancier of a place."

"Okay." Josh was intrigued. "Any hints?"

"Nope."

Josh chuckled. "Fine. Keep your secrets. See you tonight."

"See you tonight."

Erica was waiting in the lobby of her hotel when Josh arrived at seven-fifteen. She was wearing a hunter-green dress with black boots that came up just below the knee. When she saw Josh, she finished buttoning up her overcoat and walked toward him.

"Hi," she said.

"Hi," he responded. "Where are we heading?"

Erica led him back to the front entrance. "I have reservations for seven-forty-five at a French restaurant over on

Place Des Ternes. It's only two blocks north of here. I thought it might be nice to experience some proper French cuisine this time."

"I like that idea. What are they known for?"

"Seafood and bistro foods," Erica replied, as they crossed the street and headed north.

"Sounds terrific."

They arrived at the restaurant about ten minutes later, just as the winds picked up. They were early for their reservation, so they waited in the bar until their table was ready. Josh ordered them both a cocktail, and when one of the stools at the bar opened up, Josh gestured for Erica to sit.

He is a gentleman, she thought as she unbuttoned her coat and sat down.

It was too noisy in the bar to talk, so they sipped their cocktails and listened for the hostess' announcements. When they heard Erica's name called, Josh followed her to the hostess stand.

They were seated near the front windows. Josh deposited their jackets and scarfs in an empty seat and then sat across the table from Erica.

After reviewing the menu, he said, "There are too many things on this menu that I like. How am I supposed to choose?"

"I have the same problem when I come here," Erica said. "But since I'm here with you this time, how about this? If we can narrow down what we want to two things, you order one, I'll order the other, and we'll share?"

Josh smiled. "I love that idea."

Erica beamed. Then she said, "The only problem is, we have to narrow down what we want to just two items."

After several minutes of discussion, they finally agreed on a fish dish and a beef dish, and a shellfish appetizer platter. When the waiter came to take their order, Josh ordered for both of them. Erica wanted a glass of wine with her meal, and Josh ordered an entire bottle for them to share.

After the waiter left, Josh said, "I can't believe all the Christmas decorations we passed on the way here. I've never seen a city decorate so lavishly before."

"Paris loves Christmas," Erica commented. "It's one of their national pastimes. I'm hoping you're free this weekend. I want to take you to some of the Christmas marketplaces around the city. They'll blow you away with the decorations, the food, and the gifts they have for sale. I do most of my Christmas shopping at marketplaces like the ones here."

Josh nodded. "I should be free. Sounds like something I don't want to miss."

"Trust me, you don't."

The waiter delivered the appetizers, which were served in a large metal bowl filled with crushed ice. On one side were oysters on the half-shell, on the other side was peel-and-eat prawns, and in the center were crab legs and crab claws. Lemon slices on tiny forks stood out from the ice, and three metal dishes with different kinds of cocktail sauce surrounded the crab claws.

Josh and Erica attacked the appetizers with gusto.

The waiter reappeared with their bottle of wine and two glasses, poured a portion into each glass, and disappeared again.

"This is so good!" Josh said as he dipped another prawn into the cocktail sauce dish closest to him. "I never cared much for prawns, but these are incredible."

"The French are good at their seafood," Erica said, taking a bite of the crab. "Growing up in the Virginia and Maryland area, I was raised on crab. This is completely different, but it's still good."

After the appetizers had been devoured, the waiter brought their meals to the table. Erica had selected the beef dish, and Josh had ordered a fish dish. When the waiter left, Erica moved the two plates to the center of the table so she and Josh could share everything.

The food was excellent, and when the waiter brought the dessert menu, Erica said, "I'm stuffed, but if you want to split something, I'm game."

Josh noticed a dessert sampler that had small portions of five of the most popular desserts. He ordered that and handed the menu back to the waiter.

"Good choice," Erica noted. "Small portions, and we get to experience multiple flavors on one plate."

"Exactly," Josh agreed.

As they waited, Josh asked, "Any luck getting to see Janvier?"

Erica's shoulders slumped. "None. How's your project going?"

"It's going well," Josh replied. "There's a lot to review and research, but some common themes are emerging. That'll help when it comes time to craft the recommendations."

Erica nodded. "That's good. At least one of us is getting the job done."

"I'm sure you'll find a way in," Josh assured her. "Jenevieve's going to be out of the office tomorrow and Friday. Whoever is handling Janvier's calendar in her absence might be easier to convince to put you on his schedule. Can't hurt to try."

Erica brightened up. "Thanks for the tip. I'll call tomorrow and see what happens."

After paying for dinner, they left the restaurant and walked back to Erica's hotel. The wind was blowing much harder, so they walked quickly.

Josh thought about Erica's problem. *I wonder if there's something I can do to help her get to Janvier. I have a meeting on Friday with Étienne Laurent to review my progress, and I know we'll be discussing some of the expansion plans. That should open the door to talking about office space, and maybe he can help get Erica in the door if I recommend her services. It's worth a try, and whether or not anything comes from it, at least I helped a friend in need.*

He glanced at Erica, who had her head down to keep the wind out of her face. *Probably best if I don't say anything until after I've talked to Laurent. No sense getting her hopes up if I can't find a way to mention her on Friday.*

They reached the hotel and entered the lobby, which was quite warm. Erica unbuttoned her coat and saw Josh smiling. "Why are you smiling like that?"

"No particular reason," he replied. "I just had a happy thought."

"Care to share it with the rest of us?"

"Are you free for dinner on Friday?"

"You want to spend Friday night, all day Saturday and all day Sunday with me?"

"Of course," Josh replied. "From what you've told me, we've barely scratched the surface on Christmas-related things to see and do here in Paris, and Christmas is only eleven days from now."

Erica nodded. "Good point. Okay, we'll have dinner on Friday, and we can use the time to talk about what we're going to do this weekend."

"Great!" Josh hugged her and gave her a kiss on the cheek. "I guess I should head back to my hotel… unless you have different rules for third dates that I should know about."

"Unfortunately, no," Erica said with a grin. "But you'll be the first to know if any of the rules change."

Josh laughed. "No pressure. I'll call you Friday."

"Talk to you then," she said.

Josh left the lobby to hail a cab, and Erica watched him until he got into a cab and drove away.

After he was gone, she rode the elevator up to her room. Her mind was spinning. *What's wrong with me? I can't stop thinking about him. This has gone way beyond just using someone to get to a target. I think I'm starting to have feelings for Josh. Do I cut it off now, or do I let it play out on the chance that he can give me an in with Janvier? I know what Aimee would say, so I'm not going to discuss this with her. The right thing to do is to walk away and disappear from Josh's life. Yes, that's definitely what I should do...*

She entered her room and locked the door behind her. She leaned back against the door and stood in the darkness. *But that's not what I'm going to do, is it? Part of me wants to see if he can help me get in with Janvier, and part of me wants to see if Josh and I have something more between us... more than that of an art liberator and a useful idiot. He's charming, he's a gentleman, and he's done nothing to pressure me. He's the exact opposite of every other man I've encountered since before college. And even then, they weren't as ruggedly handsome as Josh is. I just have to remember that the job comes first. If I can do that, then I won't make any mistakes.*

Erica took off her coat and hung it in the closet next to the door. She turned on the lights and walked into the bathroom. Staring at herself in the mirror, she thought, *You had better not forget your rules. You made them to keep you safe, and starting a real relationship with Josh is dangerous. If you start down that road, the complications just multiply. Don't do it!*

She splashed water in her face. *But is it too late to stop it?*

Josh couldn't get Erica out of his mind as he rode back to his hotel. *She's the most beautiful, interesting, charming, and*

intelligent woman I've ever met. She has gone out of her way to keep me from being alone over Christmas, and even though I'm sure it's keeping her from being alone, too, her warmth and friendliness feels like more than just not wanting to be alone. I think there might actually be something growing between us. I want to do something to show my appreciation, but what? Maybe I'll find something this weekend when we get together.

Josh watched the lights of Paris outside the cab's window. *This is the first time I've felt close enough to someone to actually consider the possibility of a true relationship. Strange that I had to come to France to meet the American of my dreams. It kinda scares me, but it excites me at the same time. I wish I knew how she felt. I don't want to assume something's there when it's not, but I know that I'm falling for her. It's been so long... I hope I don't screw this up.*

Erica checked her email and saw one from Aimee. She opened it, and it was a list of tenants with offices in The Carpe Diem building, along with their contacts.

I'll start contacting them tomorrow and see if I can find another way into that building, in case Josh doesn't help me.

Shortly after noon on Friday, Josh knocked on Étienne Laurent's door. "Are you ready for our meeting?" Josh asked.

Laurent looked up, smiled, and nodded. "Come in, Josh." He gestured toward the conference table, where lunch had been set up. "Let's eat while we discuss your project status."

Josh sat at the table, and Laurent joined him. As they started eating, Laurent asked, "So, how is your work coming along?"

"Quite well, so far," Josh replied, swallowing a bite of chicken cordon blue. "I have a question, though."

"What is that?" Laurent asked.

"As part of the streamlining plan to help The Janvier Group grow via additional acquisitions, I couldn't help but notice that the company has a lot of office space spread around Paris and northern France. Most of the offices are legacy spaces brought over from previous acquisitions, but many of them carry high rents. Those euros can be better spent on acquisitions if you consolidate those offices and terminate some of the leases. I checked, and while there is no open space in this building, there is reasonably priced office space in this district that you could look into."

"Any new space would have to be configured to meet our particular needs," Laurent pointed out.

"That's true," Josh said. "And some of the space in this building could use some reconfiguration as well. Synergy through Proximity is a term I've heard several times since I've been here, but I don't think the proximity is working very well. Departments are spread out all over the place. I think a careful reexamination of the company's overall office space utilization could be financially beneficial, and if it's done with an eye on the future acquisitions, it could help integrate those acquisitions faster and more cost-effectively."

Laurent took a sip of wine, looking at Josh thoughtfully. "I see your point. Is that something you could include in your services, or would it just be part of your proposals?"

"It's not my area of expertise… but it happens that I know someone here in Paris who does that kind of work. I haven't worked with her before, but I know her socially, and she and her company might be worth looking into. I can provide her contact information, if you're interested in pursuing this."

Laurent nodded. "Do that, and see if you can find out what her schedule is like early next week. If she's not taking off for the holidays, perhaps she'd be willing to meet with me so we could start looking at our real estate utilization early in the New Year."

Josh smiled. "I'd be happy to. I'll reach out to her when I get back to my office, and I'll let you know as soon as I connect with her."

Laurent made a note of that in his notebook. "Excellent. Now let's discuss some of your other findings."

Josh called Erica as soon as he left Laurent's office.

"Hi, Josh!" Erica said when she answered the phone.

"Hi, Erica. What does your schedule look like Monday or Tuesday of next week?"

"You mean for dinner?"

"No, I mean during the day. I mentioned you to Étienne Laurent in my last meeting. He's the head of Operations for The Janvier Group. He's interested in talking to you about consolidating and reconfiguring the company's office space."

There was a pause, and then Erica said, "You're kidding. You got me a meeting with The Janvier Group?"

"Sure," Josh said casually. "I don't know if you'll get to meet with Janvier himself before the end of the year, but at least this will get you in the door. And if you're contracted to evaluate *all* of Janvier's office space, you'll surely have the chance to meet him personally at some point."

"This is unbelievable," Erica gushed. "Thank you, Josh. You have no idea how happy this makes me. Here I've been wracking my brains trying to figure out how to get past the front doors. And it turns out that it's you who provided the solution. My boss will be thrilled. Hell, *I'm* thrilled! I don't know how to thank you."

"It's my pleasure," Josh said. "You've been so kind to

me… I'm just happy that I found a way to do something nice for you."

"You certainly did! Tell your client that I'm free all day Monday and Tuesday."

"How about Monday at ten in the morning?" Josh suggested.

"That works perfectly. I'll be there. Hey, are we still on for tonight?"

"I hope so," Josh replied. "What do you have in mind?"

"Something a little different," Erica said. "Dress casually and very warm. Oh, and wear your best walking shoes. We'll be outside and on foot for most of the evening."

"Okay. I'll call you when I'm on my way, okay?"

"Great," Erica said. "See you tonight. Bye."

"Bye."

Josh put away his phone, sent Laurent a quick email confirming his meeting with Erica at ten on Monday morning, and then started looking at the latest batch of reports that Laurent's staff had compiled for him.

Erica ended the call and did a happy dance in her hotel room chair. *YES!! I knew that Josh was the best way into The Janvier Group. If my meeting next week goes well, I'll have the full run of The Janvier Group's office spaces. If I find the statue there, it'll be easy enough to liberate it for the client. If not, then I'll know it's at his primary residence, and I can devote my time figuring out how to breach his security there.*

She dialed Aimee's number.

"What's up, Erica?" Aimee asked when she answered the call.

"I think I've found a way in at The Janvier Group!"

"How?" Aimee asked.

"Remember that guy I met who works there?"

"Yes." Aimee's voice betrayed her lack of enthusiasm.

"He got me an interview with Janvier's head of Operations on Monday. If that guy likes what I have to say, I'll have the run of all of Janvier's offices."

"And if the statue isn't there?" Aimee asked.

"Always the pessimist," Erica joked. "If it's not at the office, I'll know it's at his residence, and I can concentrate on how to gain entry there."

"Well, you're finally making progress, so congratulations. By the way, that Josh guy's background check came back clean. Any luck with the list of contracts I sent you for the other companies with offices in that building?"

Erica chuckled. "Figures you'd run a background check. As for the contacts, I called them, and they all said the same thing."

"What?"

"'Call back after the first of the year.' I warned you this wasn't going to be an easy assignment," Erica reminded her. "And whether or not the item is at the office or the home residence, we have to eliminate the possibilities one at a time. This is the first of many steps, but it's a necessary first step."

"Agreed," Aimee said. "Any luck with Janvier's neighbors?"

"Not yet. I want to be certain that a roof penetration is even possible before I spin my wheels trying to get one of his neighbors to take me on as a client. That'll have to wait until I examine the security installation, renovation plans, and whatever his interior designer did when he bought his home."

"I understand. Well, I'll alert the client that you're making progress but you need more time. You be careful, and remember what I said about that Josh guy."

"That his background check came back clean?"

"No," Aimee snapped, "that it's dangerous getting involved with him."

"I won't forget. But you have to admit I was right about him."

"You can remind me of that after you've recovered the statue and are safely out of Paris."

"Fine," Erica said. "I'll call you next week after my interview."

Erica ended the call. *I'm going to be spending all weekend with Josh, starting tonight. I'll need to keep my wits about me so I don't do something foolish... or stupid. And I absolutely can't drink champagne. Every time I do, I end up doing something really stupid, and I don't need that right now. Stay sober, show him a good time, string him along until I find the statue and recover it, and then disappear forever. That's the way Aimee wants me to play it, so that's what I should do.*

She thought about Josh for a while. *But I REALLY like him. Can I just walk away when the assignment is over?*

She stared out her hotel window. *I don't think so.*

Josh arrived at Erica's hotel shortly after six on Friday evening. She was waiting in the lobby for him.

"What's the plan for tonight?" Josh asked.

Erica smiled. "Tonight, we're going to look at the Christmas lights and decorations along the *Champs-Élysées*. There's a Christmas Carnival and Market at Tuileries Garden near *Place de la Concorde*, and there will be a lot of places serving food and Vin-chaud."

"What's Vin-chaud?" Josh asked.

"It's mulled wine, made with hot red wine mixed with sugar, orange or other fruits, and spices like cinnamon. It's one of Parisians' favorite winter beverages."

As they walked out the hotel's main entrance and headed south toward the Arc de Triomphe, Erica said, "We'll start at the

Arc de Triomphe, then head along the *Champs-Élysées* to the *Place de la Concorde* and then swing over to Tuileries Garden. There are other places we should go before Christmas, but we'll save them for another time."

"We have all weekend," Josh noted.

"Exactly. No sense trying to do Paris all in one night."

The crowds grew as they approached the *Champs-Élysées*. "I guess Friday nights are the same all over the world," Josh commented.

"Everyone out to have a good time," Erica responded. "Young lovers out to see the sights." They passed an older couple arm in arm. "And older lovers out as well. It's Christmas in the City of Love."

They reached the *Champs-Élysées* and turned east. Erica took his hand—without thinking—so they wouldn't get separated by the people scurrying here and there.

"You should see this place on New Year's Eve," Erica said as they walked. "The avenue is closed to traffic, and the party starts after sundown and goes until well into the morning. The crowd on the avenue is at least as large as the ones in Times Square or the Mall in Washington on the Fourth of July."

"Sounds like this is the place to be on the thirty-first."

"We can, if you want," Erica said. "Be here, that is."

"I like that idea," Josh said.

Erica nodded. "Good."

They walked along the sidewalk, looking at the sights. Every tree sparkled with lights along the branches, and lights decorated the storefronts as well. For Josh, it was a magical experience.

When they finally reached *Place de la Concorde*, they walked toward Tuileries Garden—next to the Louvre—to experience *La Magie de Noël*, the Magic of Christmas. The Christmas themed carnival and market grew out of the Christmas markets formerly along the *Champs-Élysées* and had become one of the largest and most popular Christmas Markets in Paris.

As they approached Tuileries Garden, Josh saw a huge Ferris wheel in the distance. He pointed to it, and Erica nodded.

"That's where we're going," she confirmed. "Prepare yourself for quite an adventure."

When they reached the carnival and marketplace, Josh was amazed. The smells from dozens and dozens of food vendors were intoxicating. The sounds from the carnival rides and games reminded Josh of the amusement parks he frequented as a child. And the wares from the various sellers on display beckoned him forward. He suddenly forgot how tired he was from the long walk. All he wanted to do was see and sample everything that the market had to offer.

Josh and Erica set off in search of something to eat, but there were distractions everywhere they looked. The hundreds of Swiss-Chalet-styled booths were filled with unique gifts, sweet and savory treats, and hot and cold beverages of all sorts.

They found foods of every type to sample, and the Vinchaud was warm and delicious. They bought dozens of gifts for family and friends, and they stuffed themselves with delicacy after delicacy. They opted to forego the rides and the ice-skating rink, but there were more than enough things to see and do to keep them occupied.

After several hours of exploring the market, they were both carrying several shopping bags filled with gifts they had purchased from the vendors. They were also stuffed from all the food they had eaten, a bit tipsy from the wine, and tired from the long walk.

"Do you want to call it a night?" Erica asked.

"I'm not ready to leave you," Josh replied. "I just want to get off my feet for a while. I imagine we're going to be doing a lot of walking tomorrow, right?"

Erica nodded. "I had planned to take you to the Eiffel Tower Christmas Market. And then, if you're not too tired, to the

Marché de Noel Notre Dame, across the Seine from the cathedral in Square Viviani. There's also a huge market near your hotel. The La Defense Christmas Market on the Esplanade is the biggest in Paris. We can save that for Sunday, since I want to take you to the Paris Festival of Lights over in the Latin Quarter tomorrow night."

Nearby, Josh saw an empty park bench close to an outdoor propane heater. He gestured toward it, and they sat quickly before another couple could come along and grab it. They sat close to each other, sharing the warmth, with their shopping bags on either side of them. Josh put his arm around Erica's shoulder, and they sat there for over an hour, people watching and talking about the Christmas traditions from their childhoods.

"We used to drive around the various neighborhoods in the ritzy Atlanta suburbs and look at the Christmas displays," Josh said. "Every Christmas Eve, we piled into the car with hot chocolate and blankets, so we could ride with the windows down and listen to the music some of the light shows had. Then we'd go home, make popcorn, open one present, and then go to bed."

Erica smiled. "We usually stayed in on Christmas Eve, watching Christmas movies and eating gingerbread. Since my parents were athletes and fitness nuts, it was the only time all year that we could binge eat sweets. To this day, I feel guilty if I eat sweets and it's not Christmas Eve. That doesn't stop me, of course, but I feel guilty anyway."

"You didn't eat candy at Halloween?" Josh asked.

Erica shook her head. "No, and we were the house that all the other kids avoided on Halloween. Mom and Dad only gave out healthy treats that no one wanted. I got stuck eating most of the leftovers, and I hated Halloween until I went off to college and got to experience a real Halloween for the first time. Now, I love it, but I still feel guilty."

"You seem remarkably fit, so clearly the sweets you do eat haven't ruined your figure."

Erica beamed. "Thank you for the compliment. I try to stay in shape; I just don't get as obsessed about it as my parents did. For me, it's a part of my lifestyle, not my entire lifestyle."

Josh gazed into Erica's eyes, and she returned his gaze. Before either of them knew what had happened, Josh leaned in, he pulled her closer with the arm around her shoulder, and Erica's lips met his.

When their lips finally parted, they had no idea how long they had held that embrace. "Was it okay that I did that?" Josh asked.

Erica cocked her head to one side, starting at him. "No, it's not all right."

"Why not?" he asked, concerned that by moving too quickly he had blown his chances with her.

"Because it ended too soon," Erica purred. She put both of her arms around his neck and pulled him in for another kiss. He didn't resist.

As they kissed, Josh had the sensation of floating, as if her kiss was propelling him to heaven. Time stood still until he felt himself returning to earth. When their lips parted, he had to remind himself where he was.

"That was amazing," he said softly.

"I'm glad you liked it," Erica said, flushed. She looked at her watch and said, "We should probably call it a night."

"Do you want me to get us a cab?" Josh asked. "I can drop you at your hotel on the way back to mine."

Erica nodded and smiled. "Good idea."

Josh hailed a cab and helped Erica get all of her shopping bags into the back seat with his. He then gave the cab driver the address of both hotels, and soon they were heading toward the Hotel Elysées Ceramic.

When they reached the hotel, Josh helped her out of the cab and grabbed her shipping bags for her. "What time do you want me to pick you up tomorrow?" he asked.

"How about nine-thirty? That way we can get there just after the Eiffel Tower's Christmas Market opens, and we can eat lunch there. We'll plan the rest of the weekend as we go, okay?"

"Perfect." He gave her a quick kiss and said, "See you tomorrow."

Erica smiled. "See you then."

Josh watched her enter her hotel and head for the elevators. Then he got back into the cab. As the cab headed for Hôtel Mgallery Nest Paris, Josh couldn't help but think about kissing Erica along the *Champs-Élysées*. *I'm definitely falling for her.*

Erica hurried up to her room. As soon as she put down her shopping bags, she removed her coat, threw it on the bed, and sat down next to it with her head in her hands.

What am I doing? What am I doing? What am I doing?

I know better than to let it get this far. Yes, I got caught up in the moment, and it was a beautiful moment, but I can't do this. I can't fall for a guy that I'm going to have to use and then discard to get the assignment done. It's no good for me, and it's no good for him. I don't want to see Josh get hurt because of me. It's not right, and it's not fair. He deserves better.

But he's clearly falling for me, and I'm falling for him. So, what do I do? He's the nicest guy I've ever met. I love the way he treats me, and I love that he's putting no pressure on me. He's just letting things happen as they happen. Yes, but look at what's happening. This has moved way past casual. Things are getting serious, and I don't want it to end. What do I do?

CHAPTER 4

The next morning, Josh walked through the entrance to Erica's hotel at nine-twenty-five. She arrived in the lobby a few minutes later, looking flushed.

"Are you all right?" Josh asked.

Erica smiled. "Of course. I just didn't sleep well and got a late start. Shall we head over to the Eiffel Tower?"

Josh nodded. He hadn't slept well either, but he said nothing. He wasn't sure how to tell her that he had stayed up most of the night thinking about her. *I don't think we're ready for that particular conversation yet.*

They took a cab to the *Champ de Mars*. Once they arrived, Josh paid the driver, and Erica took his hand. Josh didn't even question this.

Eric led him to the Christmas Market, and Josh was amazed at its size and the number of things to see and do. They spent the next several hours there, shopping and enjoying each other's company.

"I can't get over how many different varieties of Vin-chaud there are," Josh commented as he savored his third order of mulled wine that morning.

Erica was enjoying a Vin-chaud that had been made with cranberries. "That's why you should never miss the opportunity to sample some. It may have the same name as something else you've tried. It may even look the same, but each individual gives the dish or beverage its own unique twist. It's what makes Paris a foodie's paradise."

"I'm beginning to understand that," Josh responded. "Ah well, when in Rome…"

Erica pointed south. "Rome's that way."

Josh laughed. "You know what I mean. What I should have said is: When in Paris at Christmas, one must sample all of the delicacies possible, just as the Parisians do."

"Better. You don't want to start mixing French and Italian customs together in the same place, especially given their rivalry over wines."

"Noted," Josh conceded, finishing his Vin-chaud. "Almost time for another one of these."

Erica looked at him sharply. "Eat something first, will you? Otherwise you'll be a tipsy mess before midday."

Josh nodded. "Lead on."

Erica laughed and escorted him to a nearby food vendor, selling rolled crepes filled with chicken, asparagus, and cheese in a hollandaise sauce. They each ordered three of the crepes and ate them as they walked and shopped.

"I have never had so much fun at Christmas time," Josh said as they made their way through the market. "Thank you for everything you've done for me."

"My pleasure," Erica replied, finishing her last crepe. "But we're not done yet. And, believe me, it's not as much fun doing all this alone. Thank *you* for being willing to join me. It does make the holiday season much more enjoyable."

After seeing all they wanted to see at the Eiffel Tower Christmas Market, they took a cab to Square Viviani—on the North Bank across the Seine from Notre Dame de Paris—to experience the *Marché de Noel Notre Dame*. It was the first time Josh had ever seen the cathedral in person, and even though they were standing across the river from the magnificent structure, Josh was awed at the beauty of the architecture.

They walked through the marketplace, sampling foods and drinks. Josh was particularly interested in the tents where local artists were displaying their paintings and sculptures.

"You know, if I actually had a home somewhere, I'd decorate it with this art," Josh confided to Erica.

"Me, too," Erica said. "That's the curse of the nomadic life. We have no place to put and display… stuff. At some point I'll need to settle down, but until then, if I can't wear it, eat it, or use it in my work, there's no point in buying it."

"I agree," Josh said, "But that's a depressing way to look at things, isn't it?"

"It's the nature of the life we've chosen. The work provides compensations, but no life. To have a life, one must sacrifice the compensation needed to enjoy it."

"And yet, compensation without a life to enjoy it is no different than not having any compensation at all," Josh remarked.

Erica looked at him. "I never thought about it that way before. You're right. What good is compensation without a life?"

"It's no good," Josh stated. "That's why there comes a point when you have to decide to either never have a life outside of work, or to walk away from your career in order to have a life. It's that easy, and it's that hard."

"Are you reaching the point of having to make that choice?" Erica asked.

"Oh, I've been avoiding the choice for years, but yes, I'm rapidly reaching the point where the job just isn't enough for me anymore. Most of the income I've earned is just sitting in banks or in investments. I spend very little on myself that isn't reimbursed from my clients. But what good is having all that money tucked away, if I never have time to actually use it for something? I've been thinking that this assignment might be my last, and I have to say that if that's true, you've made it the best possible assignment on which to end my career. I thank you for that."

Erica blushed as she looked down. When she lifted her head again, she said, "You've given me a lot to think about, Josh." Seeing that the sun was setting, she said, "If you're done looking around here, why don't we head over to Paris Festival of Lights in the Latin Quarter? It's not far."

"Okay."

Erica took out her phone, accessed the website for *Festival des Lumières,* and purchased two passes to the event. Then she led Josh back to the main street, where they hailed a cab for the six-minute ride to *Place Valhuburt*, the entrance to the festival.

"Every year, the theme of the festival is different," Erica explained, "usually related to endangered species. This year, the focus is on tiny animals and their habitats. The huge sculptures all light up, and it's an incredible sight."

Erica flashed the QR Code on her phone at the entrance, and she and Josh were allowed to enter *Jardin des Plantes*, considered the most beautiful gardens in Paris. Walking through the displays was one of the most incredible sights that Josh had ever seen.

"You've been here before?" he asked.

Erica nodded, holding his hand. "I was here for the first year. I hear it gets bigger each year, and looking around, I believe it. This is much larger than the other one I saw."

It took over an hour to see all of the light exhibits in the gardens, and as they left the festival to catch a cab back to Erica's hotel, they were both exhausted, but very happy, with all they had done that day.

As they waited their turn in the taxi queue, Josh asked, "So tomorrow, you're coming over to my hotel, right?"

"That's right. I'll pick you up, and we'll head over to the Esplanade and the last of the Christmas Markets we'll hit this weekend."

"What time?" Josh asked.

"How about noon?" Erica suggested. "We can lunch at the market, and then we can decide what to do about dinner."

"Perfect. That'll give me time to rest up."

Erica laughed. "We won't be doing as much walking tomorrow as we did today."

Josh smiled. "Good. I need to have some strength left in my legs for work on Monday."

When it was their turn for a taxi, Josh gave the driver the name of both hotels, and soon they were heading toward Erica's. When they arrived, Josh helped her out of the cab. When she turned to face him, he leaned in, and soon they were kissing. They would have held their embrace for much longer, but the cab driver reminded Josh that he didn't have all night to wait for him. Josh and Erica laughed, and Josh watched her disappear into the hotel lobby before getting back in the cab for the ride to his own hotel.

As he watched the lights of Paris through his cab's window, he thought, *What an incredible day!*

Josh was waiting in the lobby the next morning just before noon. When Erica's cab pulled up, he exited the lobby to meet her. She opened the door and slid across the seat, making room for him.

"Good morning," he said, giving her a kiss on the cheek.

Erica beamed. "Good morning, Josh. Ready for today?"

Josh nodded. "I think so."

The cab driver dropped them off at the Esplanade near the office building where The Janvier Group was based. Hundreds of tents were lined up side by side, forming streets that serpentined all along the Esplanade.

"It's not as beautiful as the three we've already seen, but

it's impressive," Josh noted.

"It's big," Erica said. "I don't know about you, but I'm hungry. Let's find the food tents and then see what else this place has to offer."

Josh agreed, and they set out to find their lunch.

After they had eaten and toured almost half of the booths, Josh remarked, "This is so different from what we've seen already. The other three were charming, and the items for sale reflected the charm of Paris and the warmth of home and family. These items look more like something you'd display in an office. There's no warmth, no charm."

"I agree," Erica said. "Do you want to get out of here?"

"Do you mind?" Josh asked.

"Not at all," she replied. "I agree this place isn't as nice as the others we've seen." Looking around, she asked, "What do you want to do next?"

"Spend time with you," he replied.

Her smile warmed Josh's heart. She put a finger to her lips, and then she said, "Do you like museums?"

"I love museums," Josh replied.

"Wanna go to the Louvre?"

Josh nodded. "I'd love to."

They walked back to the street, hailed a cab, and were soon heading east toward the famous museum that had once been the palace of kings.

As they stood in the queue to enter the museum, Josh's excitement grew. "I've always wanted to come here."

"Me, too," Erica said. "I hear it can take days to see it all. Is there anything in particular you want to see?"

Josh's shoulders slumped. "I don't know. Between the great works of art, the Greek and Roman sculptures, the Egyptian artifacts, and the remnants of the French Monarchy, I'm not sure I could choose what to see and what to save for another visit."

Erica nodded. "Well, at least we have a list to start with.

Let's see what we can get to today, and if we don't get to see it all, we'll come back another time."

The queue began moving, and Josh held out his hand. Erica took it, and they walked together toward the entrance.

As it turned out, the museum was not as crowded as the queue implied. They were able to visit a number of galleries with priceless masterpieces adorning the walls. They also got to see the Greek and Roman statues, and the Egyptian artifacts, but they ran out of time before they before they could see the treasures of the French monarchy or the other exhibits.

"We'll come back after the first of the year," Erica promised. "There's so much to see, it'd be a shame not to see as much as we can."

"I agree," Josh said. "It's a date."

They had dinner at one of the restaurants inside the Louvre, which had great views of the grounds and gardens. After dinner, as they exited the Louvre, they saw the lights of *La Magie de Noël* at *Jardin des Tuileries* in the distance, but they decided to walk along the Seine River instead of returning to the carnival and market.

The lights reflecting off the water, and the cruise boats gliding along the river, made the night appear enchanted. Josh began to understand why so many people came to Paris to find love. Glancing at Erica, he knew that he was well beyond infatuation, but he wasn't certain if he loved her. He wasn't even sure that he truly knew what love was anymore, but she was as close as he had come since college.

The wind picked up, and he let go of her hand. He put his arm around her waist and pulled her close. She put her arm around his waist, too, and they walked along the river, simply enjoying each other's company.

"Can you believe that a week from today is Christmas?" Josh said after a while.

"No, but you're right. Any plans?"

"Not yet, but I hope whatever they are, they involve you."

Erica looked up at him. "Why don't you let me plan something for Christmas, and you plan something for Christmas Eve?"

"Whatever I plan will probably end up being your Christmas present from me," Josh said. "You're impossible to shop for."

"So are you." Erica laughed. "Okay, fine. Christmas Eve will be your gift to me, and Christmas will be my gift to you."

"As long as you're okay with that."

Erica looked at him again. "What am I going to do with a present when I live out of a suitcase year-round? It's your company I want, not a gift."

"Same here," Josh agreed. "Okay, now we know that we're seeing each other next weekend. Are you free for dinner this week?"

"Let's see how my meeting Monday goes, and then I'll let you know."

"Fair enough."

They saw a cab approaching, and Josh hailed it. It pulled over, and Josh and Erica got in. When the cab arrived at Erica's hotel, Josh kissed her goodnight. "Thanks again for a great weekend."

"My pleasure." She smiled. "I'll talk to you tomorrow after my meeting."

"I can't wait. Good night."

"Good night."

Josh got back in the cab. *I really do think I love that girl.*

Erica got to her hotel room and sat in the chair next to the window, looking out at the lights below. She felt calm—more calm than she had felt since she first met Josh. *There's no sense*

fighting it. I love him. I don't know what I'm going to do about it, but I love him. The question is: Is there any way to have both him and my career, or will I have to let one go to have the other? And if so, which one will I have to give up?

Janvier stood next to "The Van der Waal Peacock" as he watched Marco's men carefully hang the long-awaited painting that finally filled the blank wall between the two windows in the west art gallery. He felt exhilaration as the men used levels to ensure that the painting was hanging correctly.

Marco turned to Janvier. "How is that, Boss?"

Janvier smiled. "Magnificent, boys. Simply magnificent."

Janvier stepped back so he could get a better sense of how the painting looked on the wall. *Rembrandt's "The Storm on the Sea of Galilee" is finally mine and in its proper place,* he thought smugly. *After years of searching and negotiating, it's finally mine.*

"Any problems with the acquisition?" he asked.

"The owner objected at first, but we made it clear that objecting was useless."

"How many?"

"Five altogether," Marco replied. "The previous owner, his mistress, who unfortunately was a witness, and three guards—two who tried to keep us out and one who tried to keep us from getting away."

"Not a bad body count for something so spectacular," Janvier said. "Someday, people will learn to accept my initial offers when I want something. They'll live longer."

"Yes, Boss."

Janvier stepped into his office and came back out with five thick envelopes. "Your pay, gentlemen, for a job well-done." He handed one envelope to each of the men.

"Thank you, Boss. You have another assignment for us?"

"As a matter of fact, I do," Janvier said. "I don't think Marseille needs two human trafficking syndicates operating out of that fair city. My trafficking business should be sufficient to meet the needs of any current and potential clients. Kindly go there and help Mr. Lavigne and his lieutenants discover the beauty at the bottom of the Mediterranean… permanently."

"Yes, sir."

"And when you're done with that," Janvier added, "head down to Palermo and provide security for three shipping containers that are heading to central Africa. They're filled with arms, and I don't want them inspected, intercepted, or touched. I'll alert Toussaint to be on the lookout for you. Do whatever he needs you to do to protect that shipment."

"Consider it done, Mr. Janvier."

"Thank you, Marco."

Marco and his men left the house, leaving Janvier alone in his art gallery, gazing happily at his newest acquisition.

Josh sat at his desk, reviewing the latest batch of reports that Laurent's staff had provided. The phone rang, and he saw that it was Laurent.

"Good morning, Étienne. What can I do for you?" he asked when he answered the phone.

"Can you come to my office for a minute?"

"I'll be right there."

Josh walked down to Laurent's office and knocked on the doorframe.

"Come in." Laurent gestured for Josh to enter the office.

"You wanted to see me?" Josh asked.

Étienne smiled. "Yes. If you don't mind me asking, are you planning to stay in Paris over the holidays?"

"Yes, I am."

Laurent reached into his desk drawer and pulled out of small folder about the same size as an airline boarding pass. "Every year, I take my wife on a Christmas Eve dinner cruise on the Seine. I booked this year's cruise months ago. This past weekend, my wife tripped on the sidewalk, sprained her ankle, and injured her shoulder. She can barely walk, let alone eat without assistance, so now I have two tickets that I can't use for a dinner cruise on Saturday night. If you're staying in Paris, would you like them? I'd hate to see them go to waste."

"I'd be happy to take them, thank you!" Josh said. *This solves my dilemma about what to do for Erica on Christmas Eve.* "What do I owe you?"

Laurent shook his head as he handed Josh the tickets. "Not a thing. By the way, do you have a tux? It's formal attire required."

Josh nodded as he accepted the tickets. "I have a tux, and it's here with me in Paris."

Laurent smiled. "Then you're all set."

Josh glanced at his watch. "Your meeting with Erica Longwood, the interior designer, is in ten minutes. Do you want me to go down to the ground floor lobby and escort her up?"

Laurent shook his head. "Our good Günter Reinhardt would not look favorably on that. He likes to intercede with all guests before they're allowed into the offices."

"What if I meet him at the elevators on this floor and escort Erica here once he's done with her?"

Laurent nodded. "That'll be fine. I'll call Günter and let him know you'll meet him and Miss Longwood at the elevators."

Josh held up the tickets. "Thanks again for the tickets. I really appreciate it."

Laurent nodded and then gestured for Josh to leave. Josh left, returned to his office, and put the tickets in his briefcase. He sent a quick text to Erica asking her to let him know when she arrived so he could meet her at the elevators. She responded a moment later that she had just arrived in the main lobby and was waiting to be escorted to the twenty-seventh floor.

Josh waited a few minutes, then he headed for the elevators. Less than five minutes later, the elevator doors opened, and Erica exited, followed by Günter Reinhardt.

"Ah, Mr. MacGregor," Reinhardt said. "Here is Miss Longwood to see Mr. Laurent. She will need to be escorted back to the ground floor when her meeting is over."

"I'll take care of that," Josh assured him.

"Very well." Reinhardt got back into the elevator and the doors closed.

"Hi!" Josh said to Erica, unable to keep from smiling.

"Hi, yourself," Erica said pleasantly. "You seem happy today."

"I'm happy to see you, and I have something special lined up for Christmas Eve. It's formal attire required, so I hope you have something suitable."

"I do," Erica confirmed. "Do you?"

Josh nodded as he used his key card to open the door into the offices. Erica walked through the door, and Josh led her to Laurent's office, pointing out his own office when they passed it.

When they reached Laurent's office, Josh made the introductions, and then he left them alone to discuss how Erica might help The Laurent Group.

Josh stopped at Laurent's secretary's desk and said, "Mr. Reinhardt asked me to escort Miss Longwood back to the ground floor when her meeting is over. Can you call me and let me know when she's done with Étienne?"

The secretary nodded, and Josh returned to his office.

An hour later, Laurent's secretary brought Erica to Josh's office. "Miss Longwood is finished with her meeting," she said, leaving Erica in Josh's care.

"Thank you," Josh said, standing.

When the secretary had left, he asked, "How did it go?"

Erica beamed. "I think it went well. There's no question I can do what he needs done, and I gave him a number of examples of where I've done similar work for other clients. He has to run it by Janvier and check my references, but if Janvier has no objections, I should get the contract and start working early in the New Year."

"Erica, that's great!"

"And it's thanks to you," she said softly.

"My pleasure," Josh replied. "I'm happy I could help. I know how important it is to you."

He led her to the elevators.

"So, what are these formal plans you made for Christmas Eve?" Erica asked.

"A dinner cruise on the Seine."

Erica started at him, open-mouthed. "How? Those things are sold out months in advance."

"A client had two tickets he couldn't use, so he gave them to me," Josh admitted. "It seemed perfect."

"It is," Erica stated. "Wow! I can't wait!"

The elevator doors opened, and they rode down to the ground floor.

"Are you free for dinner any night this week?" Josh asked as they reached the main lobby. "We should celebrate your good fortune."

"Hey, nothing's definite yet," Erica reminded him. "But I did finally manage to have a face-to-face with someone here, so I guess that's worthy of a celebration. How about tomorrow night? I'm still kind of stuffed from this past weekend."

Josh laughed. "Me, too. Tomorrow night it is. Something simple, I imagine."

"That sounds perfect to me."

Josh gave Erica a kiss on the cheek and watched her leave the lobby. Then he took the elevator back up to his office so he could finish reviewing the day's reports.

Erica called Aimee when she got to her car. "The meeting went well. Barring anything unforeseen, I should start working with The Janvier Group early in the new year."

"Nicely done, girl!" Aimee said. "And I'll admit that Josh was valuable in this instance. I still think that you should limit your involvement with him, but if he continues to help you without knowing *how* he's really helping you, then I'll be the first to admit that I was wrong about him. Just don't let it go too far, and whatever you do, don't fall for him."

"Of course not," Erica lied.

"Keep me informed. I'll draft a standard contract and send it to you, just in case Janvier wants to proceed."

"Thanks. Any luck finding the contractors, the interior designers, and the security companies that worked on Janvier's residence?"

"I think so, but I'm waiting on a few confirmations. Hacking into so many companies is slow going, and a lot of these companies don't have remote access into their systems, so I'm having to hack the government offices that oversee the renovation of historic properties. I should have the information by next week at the latest."

"That works," Erica said. "Most of the companies will be shut down between Christmas and New Year's, so it'll be easier for me to break in and get the information I need about Janvier's home. Talk soon. Bye."

After Erica hung up and started her car, she thought, *'Don't fall for him.' It's a bit late for that.*

Tuesday night, Josh and Erica had dinner at the pizza place near her hotel. With all the fancy food they'd be eating Christmas weekend, they decided that the food they grew up with was the best option.

The Janvier Group's offices were scheduled to be closed on Friday, December 23rd, so Thursday afternoon, Raphaël Janvier hosted a cocktail party at the end of the workday for his key staff. Josh was invited. The party was located in Janvier's apartment, which was connected to his office through a corridor hidden by the wall of bookcases behind his desk.

Josh had never been in one of Janvier's residences before, and he took the opportunity to look around at the priceless works of art adorning the walls. *Erica asked me if Janvier had any statues. I don't see any. I guess he prefers wall art and not standing art.*

That night, Josh meet Erica at an American restaurant that specialized in burgers and fried chicken. It was strange eating American food in Paris, but the restaurant seemed dedicated to fun, and the couple enjoyed themselves.

"I heard back from Étienne Laurent today," Erica said. "I got the contract!"

"That's terrific!" Josh exclaimed. "When do you start?"

"First of the year," Erica replied happily.

"I'm glad he got hold of you today. The offices are closed tomorrow and Monday, so you wouldn't have heard anything until Tuesday at the earliest."

"So you have a four-day holiday?"

Josh nodded, sipping his milkshake.

"We'll have to think of something to do, won't we?"

"We already have something planned for Saturday night, but I'm free on the other three days."

"Not on Sunday night, you're not."

Josh looked at her. "You have something planned that

night?"

Erica grinned. "What's the one thing you've wanted the most since arriving in Paris, but you haven't gotten yet?"

"You mean food-related right?"

Erica pretended to hit him. "Of course, I mean food."

"Easy," Josh said. "Steak."

"Right. So, that's my Christmas present to you. We're having Christmas dinner at a steak house here in Paris, and from what I hear, it's as good as anything you'll find in the States."

Josh smiled broadly. "Now that's the perfect gift, thanks!"

They continued eating. When Josh finished his burger, he said, "By the way, I was invited to the pre-Christmas cocktail party in Janvier's apartment this afternoon."

Erica froze, but tried to hide it by taking a quick sip of her drink. "Really? What was that like?"

"A typical office party, but you have to see his apartment to believe it. I've never seen paintings like that outside of a museum. I'm no expert, but they all looked priceless. I remembered you asked me once if he had any statues or figurines. I looked, but I didn't see anything art-related that wasn't hanging on the walls."

Erica nodded. "I didn't see any on the floor I visited on Monday either. Makes sense. Things tend to get knocked over and broken in offices."

Josh looked at her. "When you said we had to think of something to do during my four-day holiday, did you have something in mind?"

Erica gazed at him seductively. "Perhaps. Do you feel lucky?"

"Uh, what are you talking about, Erica?"

She laughed. "There's a part of Paris known as *Centquatre-Paris*. It's where the casinos are located. There's a great one on the *Champs Elysées* near the Arc de Triomphe. We walked past it last weekend when we were looking at the lights."

Josh nodded. "I remember. It was an impressive looking establishment."

"There are several in the area, but I thought we might try our hand there first. It's not far, and it's open from one in the afternoon until six in the morning. Care to test your luck?"

"I'm game if you are. Of course, we may have to make a side wager or two... you know, just to make things more interesting."

Erica flashed a wicked grin. "I think I can accommodate you... provided you're prepared to lose."

CHAPTER 5

s they took a cab to the casino, Erica remarked, "Since you've never been to Paris before, I'll warn you that the casinos here are different from the casinos in the States. Most of what you'll find here are only card games. You might find a few roulette wheels, but primarily it's just poker... and the occasional blackjack and baccarat tables."

"Good to know. How are you at playing poker?"

"I usually win more than I lose," Erica replied. "But I don't gamble that often. Money is too hard earned to throw it away. When I walk into a casino, I have a certain amount of money I'm prepared to lose. That's my original stake for the evening. Once it's gone, I'm through. And if I'm doing well, once I've doubled my money, I pocket my original stake and only play with the winnings until that's gone or I double my winnings again. Either way, once that happens, I'm done. That way, I don't lose too much, and I don't fool myself into thinking that I'm a great player who can keep winning all night."

"Do you play the cards or the other players?" Josh asked.

"Both," Erica said, "but you have to learn to play the other players. It's the only way to know if they're bluffing or if they believe they hold the winning hand."

"That's the hardest part for me," Josh admitted. "I know

how to give false tells about my own hands, but I'm not good at reading the tells of the other players."

"Then stay away from the high-money tables," Erica warned. "Those players are pros, and they'll clean you out before you know what hit you. I only play those tables when I'm feeling reckless."

"I'll keep that in mind," Josh said.

When they arrived at the casino, they acquired their chips from the cashier and then looked for the tables where they wanted to play. They agreed that they'd stay close to each other, but they wouldn't play poker against each other at the same table unless they were both winning significantly at their own tables.

They decided they'd start at the *Punto Banco* tables, which was a Mexican game inspired by Baccarat, where the players play against dealer, not each other.

At first, the dealer, known as the Banker or Banco, seemed unbeatable. But when Erica was dealt cards that equaled nine when added together—the object of the game—it broke the dealer's winning streak, and soon both Erica and Josh had large stacks of chips in front of them.

After an hour of doing well at the *Punto Banco* table, they decided to try the Poker 21 tables. This game, also known as Blackjack Parisian Style, had the same rules as American Blackjack, except that six decks were used.

Josh had always been good at Blackjack, and he soon had a sizeable stack of chips in front of him. Erica didn't do as well, breaking even by the time they decided to move to the Texas Hold'em tables. They found empty seats at two adjacent tables. Once seated, Josh had little time to wonder how Erica was doing. He was up against players with very different styles and skills, but in spite of that, he did well.

At one point, while the Croupier—or dealer—was changing the card decks, Josh glanced over at Erica and saw that her stack of chips had grown considerably.

Once Josh had amassed a large stack of chips, he pushed back from the table and decided to take a chance at one of the tables for more advanced players. He told Erica what he was doing, and she decided to join him.

"We've both been doing well," Erica said, "but I think it's time we played against each other. I don't like being at different tables. It's no fun."

"Will it be any fun competing against each other?" Josh asked.

"Only one way to find out," she replied. "But if it stops being fun, we agree that we'll either go to separate tables, or we'll stick to games where we're playing against the Croupier instead of other players."

Josh agreed, and they found a table that had two open seats at the opposite ends of the table.

After two hours, Erica was up thousands of euros, and Josh was holding steady with the same amount of chips he had when they first sat down at the table. There had been only one hand where it came down to the two of them for the entire pot, and Erica had come out the winner.

An hour later, though, three of the other players went all-in with their entire stacks of chips. Two players folded, leaving only Josh and Erica still betting. After they had raised each other several times, Erica went all-in with the chips she still had on the table, forcing Josh to go all-in with his chips if he wanted the chance to beat her.

When the players had to show their hands, Erica had a full house, which beat the other three players. Josh had a straight flush, and he took the pot totaling over seventy-thousand euros.

Josh and Erica decided to call it a night. The Croupier placed Josh's winnings in a rack so they wouldn't fall out, and Josh and Erica headed to the cashier's cage so they could exchange their chips.

"How did you do tonight?" Josh asked Erica.

"A little better than you did," she replied. "I kept moving chips into my purse as I kept winning, so even though you cleaned me out of the chips I had left on the table, I still have close to eighty thousand euros in chips in my purse."

"Outstanding," Josh said, impressed. "We both did well… and now have even more money that we can't do anything with."

Erica laughed. "We can always donate it to charity."

"I'd like to donate much of it to charity," Josh confided. "And I think I'll spend the rest of it on you while we're both in Paris. You're the reason I have all this money now. I never would have come here by myself."

"You don't have to do that, Josh," Erica said, sounding surprised.

"What if I want to?"

"What if I want to do the same with my winnings?" she asked.

Josh looked at her. "Then I guess we'll be having some interesting times over the next few months."

After they had cashed in their chips and had their winnings wired into their bank accounts, Josh looked at his watch. "Did you know it's four in the morning? It's Christmas Eve Eve!"

"Merry Christmas Eve Eve," Erica laughed, throwing her arms around Josh's neck and kissing him.

Josh put his arms around her and held her close. When Erica finally pulled away, Josh could tell that she did it reluctantly.

"I should probably go back to my hotel, if I want to be rested before tomorrow night. What time are you coming by to get me?"

"The cruise departs from *Port de la Bourdonnais* at eight-thirty, and returns around midnight. We can check in anytime between seven and eight. Why don't I pick you up just after seven, so we have time to get through traffic?"

"Perfect. You did say formal, right?"

"That's what Étienne Laurent said when he gave me the tickets."

Erica smiled. "Good. I've got a dress I've been dying to wear."

"I can't wait to see it."

"And I can't wait to see you in your tux."

They left the casino and caught a cab back to their hotels.

Once back in her hotel room, Erica checked her emails. The first was from Aimee, providing information about the renovation contractors, interior designers, and security system installers who had worked on Janvier's residence after he had purchased the property.

Erica checked each company to confirm that they'd be closed between Christmas and New Year's. Only the security company would be open all week.

Feeling wide-awake, she changed and went downstairs to the valet desk to have her car brought around. A few minutes later, she was heading for the renovation contractor's offices. She wanted to reconnoiter the offices of the three companies to help plan how and when to break in and find the blueprints, schematics, and other design documents she needed to plan her penetration of Janvier's residence.

It took most of the day, well into the night, and part of the next morning to investigate the three offices, identify the security they used, and develop her plans for breaking in—to obtain the information she needed on Janvier's residence—and getting back out without anyone ever knowing she had been there.

As the Saturday morning sun began shining through her hotel window, she decided she needed to get some sleep so she'd be wide awake for the river cruise with Josh that night.

Josh walked into Erica's hotel lobby at seven o'clock on Christmas Eve. Hotel patrons were dressed in their finest as they headed out for parties and dinner engagements.

The elevator doors opened, and Erica emerged, wearing a strapless, sleeveless, full-length burgundy dress. She wore a diamond necklace with matching earrings, but no other jewelry. She looked stunning.

"You look amazing," he said, wide-eyed.

"And you look incredibly handsome," she purred, running her hand along the satin lapel of his dinner jacket.

He helped her put her coat on and then donned his own overcoat. They stepped outside and moved to the end of the taxi queue. When it was their turn for a cab, Josh said, "*Port de la Bourdonnais.*"

The cab pulled away from the hotel and headed for the river port.

"I can't believe I'm finally getting to do this," Erica said, snuggling close to Josh. "I've been on the river cruises before, but never the dinner cruise."

"This will be my first time doing either," Josh said.

Traffic was heavy, but there were no major delays getting to the *Port de la Bourdonnais*, under the *Pont d'Iéna* at the foot of the Eiffel Tower. By seven-forty, they had checked in. Twenty minutes later, they were allowed to board and were shown to their table. There were Christmas decorations all around, including a large Christmas tree. The seating was on the glass-enclosed upper deck. Tables ran along the windows and in the center of the deck. Josh and Erica's table was in the forward section of the boat, giving them an unobstructed view of both banks of the river.

They ordered cocktails from the bar and watched the other passengers find their tables. "I hear there are carolers, other

68

performers, and an orchestra providing the live entertainment," Erica said.

"I saw the musicians setting up in the center of the boat," Josh commented. Changing the subject, he said, "I know this has a six-course meal ending with a *Buche de noël*, but I have no idea what the rest of the menu is going to be."

Erica glanced at the Champagne cooler standing next to the table. "Don't let me have any Champagne," she said.

"Why?"

"Because it makes me do crazy things, and that's not something I want to do on Christmas Eve. It seems... disrespectful."

Erica didn't elaborate on what crazy things Champagne made her do, and Josh didn't press the point. "I'm sure they'll have other wine options," he said.

The carolers began singing as soon as the boat pulled away from the dock, and the dinner service began shortly after that. There was enough lighting to see the food, but it didn't detract from the views outside the windows. Paris at night was beautiful, but decorated for Christmas along the river was breathtaking. Josh and Erica said very little as they ate, enjoyed the sights, and listened to the orchestra playing.

Josh was aware of the other boats on the river, but they simply added to the charm of the evening's sights.

Once the meal was finished, and they were enjoying the last of the bottle of Rosé that Josh had ordered, Erica and Josh moved their seats closer together so they could appreciate each other's company more as they enjoyed the view.

When the boat finally returned to the dock, neither Josh nor Erica wanted to leave. When they finally stood and retrieved their coats, Josh said, "Merry Christmas, Erica."

"It's after midnight isn't it?" Erica asked.

Josh nodded.

"Merry Christmas, Josh." She kissed him, and Josh had that

floating sensation again. When they finally parted, they realized they were almost the last passengers onboard. They bundled up in their coats, exited the boat, and headed for the taxi queue.

"What are your plans for tomorrow?" Erica asked. "Besides dinner with me," she added.

"No plans yet."

"How about brunch?"

"Are any restaurants open on Christmas Day, besides for the dinner service?"

"The ones in the hotels usually are." She pulled out her phone and searched the local hotels. "The Hyatt near the Louvre is open and has a table at ten in the morning. Would you like to meet there? We can decide how to spend the rest of the day after that."

"Sounds lovely," Josh said, grateful to get to spend more time with Erica.

Erica booked the table. She smiled at Josh as she put away her phone. "Good. I was hoping we could spend time together tomorrow before dinner."

Josh put his arm around her and pulled her close to keep her warm as they waited for the next available cab.

Josh walked into the lobby of the Hyatt on *Rue de la Paix* the next morning at nine-forty-five. He didn't see Erica anywhere. He checked the restaurant, but she hadn't arrived there either. He went back to the lobby and sat down facing the main entrance to watch for her.

After five minutes, two hands covered his eyes. "Guess who."

It was Erica's voice. "I don't know," Josh said, "but I'm expecting someone, so whatever you have in mind, it had better be quick."

Erica laughed as she came around and sat next to him. "I came in the side entrance and saw you waiting for me. I decided to sneak up on you."

Josh kissed her. "Merry Christmas."

"Merry Christmas to you, too," Erica purred. "Shall we eat?"

Brunch was wonderful, and Josh was happy with Erica's suggestion. It was noon when they finished eating. After they left the restaurant, they sat in the hotel lobby and talked for a while. It was clear to Josh that Erica had something on her mind, but he decided to wait and see if she wanted to share what it was. He didn't want to force her to talk about something that she wasn't ready to tell him.

Few places were open on Christmas day, and they still had six hours to kill before their dinner reservation. Erica suggested that they hit one of the other casinos near the *Champs Elysées*, and Josh agreed.

This casino, also dedicated to poker, attracted a higher-skilled selection of players, and Josh lost his original stake in less than an hour. Because he had won so much at the first casino, he decided to give himself another stake and try again. He did slightly better this time, but by the time he and Erica needed to leave, he had only broken even and hadn't managed to win back his initial losses.

Erica did quite well with her initial stake, cleaning out a number of seasoned players. Josh began to suspect that she was a seasoned player as well.

They took a cab to Erica's hotel so she could change for dinner. She returned to the lobby wearing a hunter-green dress that stopped at the knees, a simple chain with a snowflake pendant, and matching earrings.

"You look gorgeous," Josh said, helping her put on her coat as she wrapped her cranberry-red scarf around her neck.

They took another cab to Josh's hotel. When they arrived,

he invited her up to his room. She hesitated at first, but since they were only there so Josh could change for dinner, she accepted.

When they entered his room, Erica gasped. "You have a suite?"

"It's what The Janvier Group arranged for me. I think they do enough business here to get a great rate."

Erica walked through the living room, and then she saw the bedroom on the other side of the room partition. "A queen bed? I haven't seen one in a European hotel room... ever. All I've got is a full-size that's only slightly larger than a twin, and my room is tiny. By European standards, this room is plush to the point of opulence."

"And it doesn't cost me a dime," Josh said, ducking into the bathroom to change into a suit.

Erica sat on the bed and bounced on it. "This bed is so comfortable. I'm jealous."

When Josh came out of the bathroom, she peeked inside. "This is the biggest bathroom I've ever seen in a hotel in France. Double sinks *and* a double standing shower? Now I'm really jealous."

As she followed him back to the living room, she added, "I don't even *want* to know what this room normally costs per night."

Josh chuckled. "No, you don't."

"That much?"

"Let's put it this way," Josh answered, "Your weekly rate at your hotel is probably less than this place's nightly rate. But like I said, The Janvier Group is picking up all charges, so I have no idea what their private rate is. I imagine it's better than anything you or I could get on our own."

They went back downstairs to hail a cab, and they were soon heading east toward the *Avenue des Ternes* to reach the steakhouse on *Rue Waldeck-Rousseau*.

When they arrived at the steakhouse, Josh was surprised at the art-deco interior. The colors were mostly royal blue and gold, which Josh remembered were the imperial colors of France. Glancing around the restaurant, he could see that most of the steaks were brought to the tables on wooden cutting boards, and the servers were removing the meat from the bones of the massive porterhouse and tomahawk steaks.

After they were seated and had ordered cocktails from the bar, Josh and Erica looked over the menu. The restaurant's regular menu items were available, but the special items just for Christmas dinner were printed on an insert inside the menu's cover.

Two items on the Christmas menu immediately caught Josh's attention: prime rib and chateaubriand. "What are you planning to get?" he asked.

"I was going to suggest getting the tomahawk for two," Erica replied, "but then I saw the prime rib on the menu. I think I'll get that. You?"

"The chateaubriand," Josh said. "It's my favorite cut of beef."

Erica smiled. "I guess we know what we're both getting. A word of advice: don't get an appetizer unless you're starving. Between the salad, the meat, the sides, and dessert, you won't have room for anything else."

Josh nodded. "Good point. I don't want to fill up on other things and not have enough room to finish the beef. It's what I'm here for… that and your company."

Erica beamed.

The server came over and took their orders. Erica also ordered a bottle of wine to go with the meal.

"This has been the most incredible Christmas I've ever had," Josh said once the waiter had left. "I can't thank you enough for everything you've done and showed me. It's a memory I'll cherish."

"My pleasure," Erica said. "And thank *you* for not making me spend Christmas alone in Paris. Any other time of year I wouldn't care, but Christmas… it's a season to be shared."

Josh nodded.

The salads arrive a moment later, and Josh and Erica began eating.

When the entrées arrived, the server carefully removed the bone from Erica's prime rib, and then he sliced the chateaubriand into medallion-sized slices. Each of the sides were then placed on the table in individual dishes.

Josh and Erica savored their meals and traded bites with each other. Everything was incredible, and Josh was quite happy with Erica's selection of restaurants for Christmas diner.

"I need to come back here before I leave Paris," Josh commented as he finished his last bite of meat. "You were right. This is a good as anything I've had in the States."

After the meal was finished and the bill paid, Josh went to the front of the restaurant to hail a cab back to her hotel.

Erica walked over to the bar.

"What can I get you?" the bartender asked.

"I need a bottle of champagne," she replied.

"The whole bottle?" the bartended inquired.

"Yes," Erica relied. "Unopened. No glasses."

The bartended nodded and procured a bottle from the cooler below the bar. Erica paid for it, put it in her purse, and went to the front of the restaurant to rejoin Josh.

"Do you mind if we take a detour before we call it a night?" Erica asked when she reached Josh.

"You're not suggesting going back to a casino are you?"

Erica shook her head. "No, there's one sight you haven't seen yet, and tonight is the last night it'll look this way."

Josh nodded. "Sure. I'd hate to miss any of the sights."

Erica smiled. When the cab arrived, Erica whispered the destination to the driver, and then she snuggled next to Josh in the back seat.

Josh couldn't quite make out where they were heading, but when he saw the Eiffel Tower lit up nearby, he began to suspect what Erica had in mind. "The observation deck at the Eiffel Tower?"

Erica chuckled. "You guessed it. I wanted it to be a surprise."

"It is, and you're right. We haven't been up there yet."

"It's better at night, and at Christmas it's amazing."

The cab dropped them off close to the Eiffel Tower, and soon Erica and Josh were in the elevator heading up to the observation deck.

When the elevator doors opened, a sudden gust of wind hit Erica and Josh. They walked arm-in-arm, turning their bodies to keep the wind away from their faces. The wind subsided a minute later, and Josh got his first look at the Parisian Christmas lights from above. It was breathtaking, and Josh thought it was the most romantic view he had ever seen.

"Josh?" Erica asked softly.

"Yes?"

"I love you."

Josh turned to face Erica. "You... love me? Are you sure?"

Erica nodded. "I've never been more sure... or more scared."

"Scared? Why?"

Erica looked down and then lifted her head to look at Josh in the eyes. "Because relationships and me have never worked out. I promised myself years ago that I was done with them, and I was perfectly content to keep that promise. And then you walked into my life. Now, I'm breaking that promise for the first time, and it... it terrifies me, even though I know I can't fight it anymore. I feel like I'm surrendering to some... fate, but I'm surrendering to myself." She paused for a moment. "Does any of this make sense?"

Josh smiled. "Yes, it makes sense, and I've been struggling with the same feelings. The nomadic life is hell on relationships, and mine have all ended badly. Then you walked into *my* life, and I find myself struggling between what I've always believed and what I want. But the truth is, I want *you*. I love you, too, Erica. I've wanted to tell you that, but I wasn't sure you felt the same, and I didn't want to jeopardize what we had." He gestured around them. "Of course, I never would've thought of such a romantic place to confess love. I'm glad you did that for us."

Erica leaned in, and Josh kissed her. After a minute, she asked, "So, what happens now? We both have jobs to do, and when they're done, we'll be off to another client and another assignment, assuming you or I don't walk away from our careers to explore the possibilities of having a meaningful life away from work."

"That's a good question. I don't know the answer. I guess we'll have to see where things go before we can figure that out. I'm willing to take a leap of faith, though. What about you?"

Erica nodded. "We can't unsay what we've said, so there's no choice. We see where things go, and when we know what we're willing to do to make this… this relationship work, *then* we make plans for the future. For now, we take things day by day, right?"

"Right."

Erica looked around a saw a number of patrons drinking champagne from glasses they got at the bar behind her. She pointed to the bar and asked, "Can you go get us a couple of champagne glasses?"

"Sure. Why?"

Erica pulled the bottle from her purse.

"I thought you had a rule about drinking champagne," Josh said. "Something about it making you do crazy things."

"I know. Tonight's different. Please?"

Josh left her and retuned a minute later with the glasses.

Erica carefully unwrapped the top of the bottle and popped the cork, covering it with her scarf to make certain that the cork didn't hit anyone or fly off the side of the observation deck. She filled their glasses, clinked hers against his, and said, "Here's to being in love in Paris on Christmas."

She downed her champagne in a single gulp and refilled her glass. Josh's eyebrows shot up, but he didn't say anything.

They spent the next hour looking at the sights, enjoying each other's company, and drinking champagne. Once the bottle was empty, and Josh had returned the glasses to the bar, Erica whispered in his ear. "Let's go back to your hotel."

"Okay." Josh looked at her. "Are you sure about this?"

Erica kissed him, and he felt that floating sensation return. "Yes, I'm sure," she said.

They took the elevator down to the ground and caught a cab back to Josh's hotel. They spent most of the ride back making out like a couple of college kids.

When they reached the Hôtel Mgallery Nest Paris, Josh paid the driver, and they took the elevator up to his floor.

He unlocked his door. Erica pushed him inside, took off her coat and scarf, tossed them on the nearby chair, and closed the door behind her. Josh removed his overcoat and scarf, and placed them on top of Erica's. Then he removed his suit coat.

"Come here and unwrap your present," she purred.

Josh didn't argue.

CHAPTER 6

Erica threw her arms around Josh's neck and kissed him. Her breathing deepened as she surrendered to the moment. *I know champagne removes all my inhibitions, but I've been struggling with my feelings for Josh for several days. Now, I'm giving in to what I really want. There'll be no regrets from what's about to happen.*

Erica loosened Josh's tie, removed it, and started unbuttoning his shirt. Josh found the top of the zipper on Erica's dress and unzipped it. Erica shook her shoulders, and the dress slipped off, revealing her black bra, panties, and thigh high stockings. Erica pulled off Josh's shirt, kicked off her shoes and pushed him toward the couch.

As soon as Josh was on the couch, he took off his shoes and socks. He looked up at Erica's body, illumined by the ambient nightlights in the room and the outside lights streaming through the open curtains. He knew she was attractive, but this was the first time he'd seen her lean, muscle-toned physique. He could see that she used to be a gymnast from her legs and waist, and her flat muscular stomach showed that she still stayed in shape. Her breasts were the perfect size for Josh, who didn't like overly busty women. He reached up and put his arms around her. She held his head close to her stomach.

Josh unfastened her bra. She removed it, and he began nuzzling her breasts and kissing her more sensitive areas. He cupped both breasts in his hands as he continued nuzzling her.

Erica knelt in front of him, loosened his belt, unfastened his pants, and pulled them off. She removed his undershorts next. She let her long hair fall into his lap, and as her head swayed from side to side, her hair began to arouse him, awakening a part of him that had not felt the touch of a woman in a very long time.

Erica pulled her hair back and reached for the object of her desire, feeling it grow and stiffen in her hands. *Wow! I had no idea...* Josh leaned back, enjoying the sensations.

Erica allowed her tongue and lips take over, and as her head moved up and down, Josh let out a low moan. Erica slowed her pace, and Josh's moans became deeper and more frequent.

To keep him from finishing too quickly, she began teasing him with her tongue, keeping him just at the point of arousal without pushing him over the edge. Then she stopped and stood up. She removed her stockings slowly, slipped off her panties, and straddled Josh. She rocked her hips forward and backward, rubbing him while stimulating herself. Then she rose up and came back down so that he was inside of her.

Erica experienced sensations that she had long forgotten about as she continued moving up and down. Josh's hands were on her hips, keeping her from leaning too far back and breaking the connection. His moans increased as she began moaning loudly. The first climax hit her, and her muscles from her knees to her stomach began spasming from the intensity of the pleasure she was giving and receiving. Her shoulders shook as she continued moving up and down. She began moving faster, clutching the back of the couch and allowing her breasts to rub against Josh's chest. She could feel herself climaxing again when she felt Josh release, sending waves of warmth deep inside her. She climaxed, and then she wrapped her arms around Josh and started kissing him.

After nearly ten minutes of enjoying the closeness, Erica rolled off Josh. "That was incredible," she said, still breathing deeply from the workout.

"You were amazing," Josh said softly. "I need some water. Can I get you one?"

Erica nodded. Josh got up and grabbed two bottles of water from the fridge. He took them into the bedroom. When he returned, he reached down, picked up Erica, and carried her into the bedroom. He had already turned down the covers, and he set her down on one side. He lay next to her, opened both bottles, and handed one to her.

"I thought we'd be more comfortable in here," Josh explained.

"That's good, because I'm not done with you," Erica said.

They made love three more times before dawn. As the light streamed through the living room window, Josh asked, "What are your plans for the rest of the day."

Erica propped herself on an elbow and faced him. "I'd love to spend the day with you, but I have a lot to do to get ready for next week. I should be free on Friday, and we already have plans for Saturday night."

"Ah, yes. New Year's Eve." Josh smiled. "Well, you can't leave without breakfast. The restaurant downstairs is good, but since you only have the clothes you wore last night, how about I order room service?"

"That sounds great."

Josh grabbed the room service menu, let Erica select what she wanted to eat and drink, and ordered breakfast for the two of them.

While they waited for the food to arrive, Erica showered, enjoying the huge freestanding shower in his room over the tiny tub shower in her own room.

When she finished her shower, she put on one of the hotel robes hung behind the door and joined Josh in the living room.

He had already picked up their clothes from the night before.

"Where are my things?" she asked, looking around.

"Your clothes are on the bed. Mine are back in my closet or in the laundry bag.

Erica looked into the bedroom. The bed had been made, and her clothes were neatly placed on the comforter. She put on her bra and panties, and when she heard someone knocking on the door, she quickly put the robe back on.

The room service waiter rolled in the cart with their breakfast. He placed the food and beverages on the table by the window. Josh signed the check, and then the waiter left.

Erica emerged from the bedroom and sat across the small table from Josh.

"Thanks for last night," she said. "That was wonderful. We'll have to do it again."

"I look forward to that." Josh smiled. "So, in the clear light of day, do you still love me?"

Erica smiled back at him. "Yes, I still love you."

"Good. I love you, too."

Erica took a sip of her coffee. "You know, we'll be working together starting next week. I'll be visiting the other office locations and meeting with the landlords of some other buildings in La Defense, but I'll also be working out of the same building as you here and there. Once my schedule settles down, we should look into how often we want to see each other and what restaurants in this part of the city we want to try for dinner."

Josh nodded. "That'll be great. You might even want to look into staying with me a few nights a week."

Erica beamed. "I had the same thought."

They finished breakfast, and Erica returned to the bedroom and got dressed. As she emerged from the bedroom, she said, "It's been a long time since I've had to do the walk of shame. Fortunately, I don't care what people at my hotel think."

"Another reason to keep a few changes of clothes here for

when you stay over," Josh suggested.

Erica nodded. When Josh stood to walk her to the door, she threw her arms around him and kissed him. "I'd rather stay here with you, but I can't. I'll call you during the week, and we'll make plans for Friday. And I'll be sure to bring a change of clothes with me."

"Perfect. I love you."

"I love you."

Erica turned and left Josh's hotel room. Josh watched her until her elevator arrived. Then he closed the door.

What Erica didn't tell Josh was that the work she needed to do involved breaking into three offices around the city.

When she got back to her hotel, she called Aimee.

"Merry Christmas," Aimee said when she answered the phone.

"Happy Boxing Day," Erica replied. "This is going to be a busy week. I'm going to reconnoiter the interior designer, the renovation contractor, and the security system company again tonight. If all goes as planned, I'll break into the interior designer tomorrow night, the contractor Wednesday night, and the security company on Thursday night. The security company is the only one of the three that isn't closed this week. Fortunately, their call center isn't in the same building, so no one should be there after hours."

"The security company makes me the most nervous," Aimee said.

"Me, too. They're undoubtedly using their most state-of-the-art system for their own offices, and if I can't breach it, I'll never be able to breach Janvier's house. It's not the first time I've done this, but this company's going to be a challenge. That's why I'm leaving them until last."

"Let's say you get the diagrams, notes, blueprints, and schematics you're looking for. What then?"

"I use that information to find the best way to breach Janvier's security and enter his home unobserved," Erica answered. "I need to know the floorplans and furniture placements, and I need to know how to enter the house without the alarms going off or the thug squad seeing me. Detailed information is the only way to plan this, assuming it can be planned."

"And if it can't?" Aimee asked.

"Then I'll have to find a way to acquire the item from the inside," Erica said. "Someone will have to let me into the house."

"All right. Call or text me after each break-in. I want to know that you made it out safely."

"Will do," Erica promised.

She ended the call, undressed, and crawled into bed to catch a few hours' sleep.

An hour after sunset, Erica's car was parked down the street from the security company's office. She used a night vision monocular to identify the location of every security camera on the street and where they were facing.

She drove around back where the office's parking area was located. She made notes of the placement of each camera, but she was unable to see how the staff entered and exited through the doors.

A few minutes later, the cleaning crew arrived and parked near the rear entrance to the building. Erica watched closely as the team leader, wearing a key card around her neck, used a regular-looking key to open the door. *The cleaning crew doesn't need a key card to enter the building. I should be able to pick* that lock. The key card must be for the interior doors or to move between floors. I hope that there are no biometrics used inside the building. I'm going to have to go inside their offices during business hours and look around. There are too many variables to know how to break into these offices. I'll go on Thursday. That way, if the job looks like it'll take more planning, I'll still have Friday as a back-up.

Erica drove to the interior design office and used the monocular to identify all cameras in the area. She looked at the adjacent buildings, which were all the same height. *The building on the end doesn't have any cameras in the front or back, and there are no cameras pointing at the rear corner. I can scale that wall easily, and breach the interior design office from the roof. If there are no motion detectors, it should be a piece of cake. If there are, I'll have to bypass the security control panel. Nothing new there.*

Erica then drove to the renovation contractor's office, a stand-alone building with a fleet of trucks parked behind a chain-link fence in the back. *Few cameras, no keypads, and no one wears a key card. They must keep all the tools and other valuables in the storehouse in the middle of the fenced-in area. That means that the best point of entry is the bathroom window near the rear entrance. It's too small for a guy to enter, but I can. As long as it's a simple magnetic contact alarm on the window, I can get in with my eyes closed.*

Having all the information she needed, she drove back to her hotel.

Just before midnight on Tuesday, Erica approached the offices of the interior design firm that redecorated Janvier's house after he purchased it. She kept to the shadows, making certain that none of the security cameras in the area could see her.

She was dressed in a one-piece flat-black unitard that wouldn't reflect light. It covered her body up to her neck. She also wore matching gloves, a matching balaclava mask that left only her eyes uncovered, and matching soft-soled boots. The fabric was insulated to keep out the cold, but thin enough to allow a full range of motion.

She reached the blind corner of the row of brick buildings, and used metal claws on her gloves and boots to scale the side of the building to the roof. She removed the claws and crept across the rooftops until she was on the roof of the interior design company.

The area around the roof door was covered with cigarette butts and beer bottles. After a quick inspection of the door, Erica found where the simple magnetic contact alarm circuit was located. She slipped two magnetic pieces of metal—connected by a wire—in between the alarm contacts. Then she picked the lock and opened the door. No alarm sounded.

She entered the stairway leading down to the third floor of the building and closed the roof door behind her. Using the night vision monocular, she looked for motion sensors and cameras. Finding none, she checked the third floor, which seemed mostly used for fabric storage and furniture restoration and refinishing.

She proceeded to the second floor, which contained offices and workshops, but no computers. She found the stairs to the ground floor and stayed in the shadows until she could survey the space for any alarm sensors. Seeing none, she crept between the desks, seating areas, and filing cabinets until she found the owner's office. There were no alarms on the door, so she picked the lock, entered the office, and closed the door.

There was a computer on the desk. Erica extracted a flash drive from the pouch on her waist, inserted it into one of the USB ports on the computer, and turned the computer on. The flash drive had a security bypass program on it that would allow Erica to access the computer's hard drive without knowing any passwords.

The computer booted up, and Erica began searching its hard drive. Not finding what she was looking for, she began searching the shared network drives. After twenty minutes, she found the client folders. She scrolled down until she found one titled "Janvier, Raphaël." She opened the folder and found all of the notes, plans, furniture placement charts, and other information about the updated décor of the house. *Bingo.* She inserted a second flash drive into the computer and copied the entire folder onto the drive. After making certain that she had everything she needed, she shut down the computer, removed both flash drives and put them back into her pouch, and then locked and left the owner's office.

As she passed the receptionist's desk, she saw several business card holders. Most had the names of the associates who worked in the office, but one was just a card for the company with no staff names on it. Erica grabbed a couple of the cards and put them in the pouch with the flash drives.

She made her way back to the roof. After she relocked the roof door, she removed her magnetic security bypass rig and put it in a separate pouch on her waist.

She crept across the roofs to the corner, where she had left her hand and foot claws. She put the claws back on, and after looking around to make certain no one could see her, she climbed back down the side of the building.

When she reached the ground, she removed the claws and looked around again. There was no traffic on the street and no lights coming from any nearby windows. Keeping in the shadows, she sprinted back to her car and climbed into the passenger seat. She quickly removed the boots and put on a pair of running shoes. She also pulled on a hoodie and removed the balaclava mask. She pulled on a woolen ski cap and put the boots, balaclava, and the claws into a drawstring bag. She put the bag over her shoulder, and slid into the driver's seat. Then she started her car and drove back to the hotel.

When she arrived at the hotel, she entered the lobby, looking like she had just come back from a long run. She waved to the desk clerk and took the elevator up to her room. Once there, she got undressed, put on an oversized t-shirt and a pair of shorts, and transferred all of the files from the interior designer onto her computer. She opened each of the files to make certain that the information she needed was there, and then she shut down her computer.

She sent Aimee a quick text. *"One down, two to go. No problems."*

After Aimee acknowledged the text, Erica went to bed.

Just after eleven on Wednesday night, Erica approached the offices of the renovation contractor, wearing the same outfit she had worn the night before when she broke into the interior designer's offices.

She slipped around the back of the building, making certain that none of the cameras watching the fenced-in area could see her. Just below the bathroom window, near the rear entrance, there was a pile of used scrap lumber. Erica carefully climbed to the top and examined the bathroom window. It had a simple alarm that Erica bypassed in less than a minute. She opened the window and carefully climbed through.

Once inside the bathroom, she closed the window and headed down the hallway to the offices, stopping several times to check for security sensors. Finding none, she entered the owner's office, activated the computer the same way she had the night before, and found… nothing. The only information on the computer was financial and personnel records. She found Janvier's billing invoices and copied them, but there was nothing else of interest on the computer's hard drive or on the shared network drives.

They must keep everything on paper files. Great.

Erica shut down the computer and started examining the rows of filing cabinets that filled nearly half of the main office's open spaces.

After almost an hour, she finally found Janvier's files. She removed them and set them on the floor. *It's a good thing my camera app was designed for low light photography.*

She found the file with the floorplans, spread the pages out, and photographed each one several times to make certain that all of the details were captured.

In another folder, she found notes and diagrams from the contractor's meetings with the security company. Even though the folder didn't contain details about the alarm system itself, it showed where each of the sensors and wires were located, since the contractor had to account for the security company's needs when installing the system. Erica photographed every page in this folder.

She examined the other folders, photographing anything that looked like it might help her plan breaking into Janvier's house. At one point, she heard a noise. She lay flat on the ground, covering the folders and papers with her body, working out the best route for escape. After several minutes, she heard no other sounds. She slowly stood and looked around. Seeing nothing, she continued photographing the information she needed. When she was done, she put everything back into the folders and returned the folders to the filing cabinet where she had found them.

She looked at her watch and realized she had been there nearly five hours. *Time to go.*

She looked around to make certain that everything was just the way she had found it. Then she made her way back to the bathroom. She looked out the window, and seeing no one around, she opened the window and climbed out. Then she closed the window, removed the alarm bypass rig, made sure the window was locked, and headed back to her car.

She had just reached the corner of the building when she saw a pair of headlights turning into the driveway next to her. She dropped to the ground and rolled next to the building, staying as far into the shadows as she could. The truck passed her and headed for the parking lot.

Why is someone here? Did I set off a silent alarm somehow? I'd better get out of here.

Erica peered around the corner. There were no other vehicles approaching. She leaped up and sprinted away before the driver of the truck could see her. She reached her vehicle as two more vehicles entered the contractor's driveway. *I thought they were closed this week. They must have a special job today and needed to get an early start. At least they're not here because of me.*

Erica quickly removed the boots and balaclava and put on her running clothes over the unitard. She put on her running shoes and ski cap, started the car, and drove off, passing several more vehicles heading for the renovation contractor's offices. *That was cutting things close!*

She arrived at her hotel and took the elevator to her floor. Once she entered her room, she copied all of the photographs she had taken onto her computer, examined each one, and then shut down her computer.

She texted Aimee before she went to bed. *"Two down, one to go. Wish me luck."*

Thursday morning, Erica approached the office of the security system installation company. She saw people inside, but the door was locked. She pressed the buzzer next to the door.

A man opened the front door, allowing Erica to enter.

"Good morning. My name is Gabriel Clément, the sales manager," he said. "How may I be of assistance?"

Erica handed the sales manager one of the cards she had stolen from the interior design offices on Tuesday night. "My name is Amanda Moreau. I have a client looking for a complete redesign of the two-hundred-year-old mansion he just purchased, and he wants to make certain that any alarm system he installs won't stand out or detract from the alterations to the interior that my firm will be recommending. I thought that combining our recommendations into a single proposal dealing with both the aesthetic design and the security design might help the client see that we have his best interests at heart. I'm here to gather information about what options exist in terms of security, and your company's willingness to partner with my company on a joint proposal."

Clément's eyes lit up. "I'd be delighted to discuss options with you. Who is your client, and where is the property located?"

Erica held up her hand. "I can't reveal that until I have my client's permission. But before I present this idea to him, I want to make certain that I know what I'm talking about."

Clément nodded. "I understand completely. If you'll follow me to my office, I'll show you our more popular options and provide you with enough literature on our products and services that you should have no trouble convincing your client that a joint venture between our two companies is in his best interest."

Erica smiled and followed Clément to his office. No one noticed the micro camera she placed on the side of the thermostat facing the security keypad and key card swipe next to the front door.

Clément spent the next ninety minutes presenting all of his company's most advanced products and services for wealthy homeowners in the Paris metropolitan area. He also discussed installation procedures, regular testing and maintenance services, and the system monitoring services.

At the end of their meeting, he provided Erica with stacks of product and service brochures, including testimonials from some of their most prestigious clients. Erica, pretending to be clumsy, dropped a stack of brochures, and when she and Clément bent down to pick them up, Erica removed his key card clipped to one of his belt loops. She pocketed the key card, took the stack of brochures from Clément, and followed him to the front door.

He entered his code into the keypad to open the front door, and Erica made certain not to block the view of the camera she had planted earlier. Then she grabbed the camera, thanked Clément for his time, left the office, and headed down the street to catch a cab to the parking lot where she had left her car. She knew better than to let a potential target see the car she was driving.

She drove back to her hotel to get some sleep before she had to return and break into the security company's office.

That night, after the cleaning crew had left, Erica approached the security company's rear entrance. She checked for alarm sensors just to be safe, but there were none. She picked the lock and entered a small room with keypad and a key card swipe next to the security door on the opposite wall.

Erica swiped Clément's key card. A red light flashed on the card reader. Erica tried again, and again, a red light flashed. Erica began to panic. *Did Clément discover that his badge was missing and deactivate it? What do I do now?*

She stared at the card reader for a moment in the low light. *Maybe the reader is touchy.* Using her elbow, she wiped down the surface of the card reader. She swiped the card again. This time, the green light flashed. She quickly entered the code that her camera had captured him using on the front door's keypad.

She heard the locks on the door disengage. She opened the door and entered the offices. She examined the door from the other side and was grateful that the key card wasn't required to exit the building. Only a keypad was present next to the door.

Using her night vision monocular, she looked for the alarm sensors. She saw cameras and motion sensors, but examining their placement and looking at the wear patterns on the carpet—which stood out using the night vision technology—she noticed a blind spot that ran just in front of the offices along the back wall, including Clément's. Rows of filing cabinets blocked the view of the cameras along the front wall, and the only cameras on the back wall pointed forward. No cameras pointed down along the back wall.

If I crawl along the floor, the cameras will see the office door open, but they'll never see me.

She lay flat on the floor and began inching forward until she reached Clément's office. She reached up and used the key card to unlock his door. When she heard the lock release, she opened the door and slid through. She closed it behind her, grateful that the blinds covering the one window were closed.

She went to his desk and inserted the flash drive that bypassed security into the USB port. Soon the computer was on, and Erica was searching the shared network drives for Janvier's folder.

Damn, they have a lot of clients, Erica thought as she searched folder after folder. After nearly an hour, she found the folder containing all of the information for the security system installed in Janvier's house. The folder was huge, and as Erica browsed the contents, she realized that she had never gone up against a security system as sophisticated as the one Janvier had them install for him.

She plugged in the other flash drive and began copying the folder. *This is going to be the toughest security I've ever had to breach. I hope I can find a way to get into Janvier's house undetected.*

Once the files had been copied, Erica shut down the computer and pocketed the flash drives. She took Clément's key card and dropped it under his desk. Then she crouched down next to the office door, opened it, and crawled out on her belly. After closing the office door, she inched her way back to the rear entrance. She stood and entered Clément's code into the keypad. The door unlocked, and Erica slipped through, closing the door gently behind her.

Erica crossed the small room and exited the rear entrance, making certain that the door was locked. She hugged the back wall of the building, staying in the shadows, until she reached the street. At the corner of the building was the drawstring bag she had left there. She opened it, pulled on the hoodie, removed her boots and put on the sneakers, and then removed the balaclava and put on the ski cap. She put the items she had removed into the bag, slung it over her shoulder, and began jogging back to her car, which was several blocks away.

After Erica returned to her hotel room, she uploaded the information from the security company to her laptop. She began studying the information from the three companies to find the best way to penetrate Janvier's security and find the item she had been hired to recover.

She examined the information from the interior designer and the renovation contractor first. Based on the floorplans and the placement of furniture on all seven floors of Janvier's house, she found two places where the item was most likely located. The sixth-floor renovations included tearing out most of the walls to create large rooms on either side of the central stairs. Access to the side stairs—originally used for servants and now used as the fire escape—was at the far end of one of these rooms.

The entrance to Janvier's office was at the far end of the opposite room. There was also a back staircase that went from the basement to the fifth floor.

There's virtually no furniture in these two rooms except for tufted benches, like the ones you see in a museum gallery. The walls were reinforced to prevent damage to the plaster from large paintings with heavy gilded frames. The only other items ordered for the space were custom display cases. Assuming he doesn't have the item in his office or bedroom, it's most likely in one of these two rooms on the sixth floor.

Erica then turned her attention to the security system. The more she studied it, the more agitated she became. *This bastard's thought of everything. Motion sensors, laser arrays, low light and regular cameras, pressure sensors, heat sensors... everything. From the placement of the ceiling cameras, there's a camera over each display case and painting, and other cameras trained on each painting and display case at various angles, making any unseen approach to the item impossible. I can't enter the room from the ceiling, and if I walk across the floor, the pressure and heat sensors could be triggered, not to mention the laser sensors.*

There's no way I can enter from the roof because the contractors sealed off the entrance, even though they left the door there. The windows are all bullet-proof, four-pane-thick security windows with gas pressure sensors between each pane and multiple motion alarms on each that are designed to go off if anyone attempts to use a probe to detect where the alarm contacts are located. Even with the plans showing me the alarm contact locations, any attempt to bypass a contact will set off the alarm, and there are at least a dozen contacts per window.

The back door is just as protected as the windows, and it's a steel reinforced door, so there's no way to breach the door without setting off the alarm and attracting the guards' attention... not to mention the cameras trained on all of the doors around the house. He even has cameras on the roof!

Erica went back through the security system design. *I can't breach from a neighbor's home without punching through a wall. I can't approach the house without being seen by a camera. I can't enter via the roof, a window, or the back door. Even if I did, I can't enter the galleries on the sixth floor without being detected and alerting the security guards. If I cut the power to the security system, there are back-up batteries on all of the devices. The alarms won't sound, but the cameras will still see everything that happened. And there's a generator built in to the house's power system that automatically turns on if the power is out for more than a couple of minutes. I may be fast, but I can't break in, reach the sixth floor, acquire the item, and get back out in under two minutes, especially since there are multiple places the item may be located.*

Erica shook her head. *I've never had to admit this before, but I can't beat Janvier's security. The only way inside that house is by invitation, and once inside, he'd never let me out of his sight. This is hopeless.*

She called Aimee to give her the bad news.

Aimee seemed irritated by Erica's conclusions. "We were hired to recover a stolen piece of art. You willingly took the assignment. But all you've given me is a number of reasons why you can't steal it back. So, how are you going to recover the client's property?"

"I don't know," Erica admitted. "I start working at the target's company next week, so I'll be able to search his apartment there—rule it out once and for all. If the object turns out to be there, then I can recover it. If not, then I have to find a way to be allowed into his house. I heard he throws some lavish parties. If I can secure an invitation, or if I can infiltrate his caterer, then I might be able to search the house, recover the item, and escape with it. But that's going to take a lot of luck. I'll figure something out, but at the moment, I can't think of anything that's guaranteed to work."

There was a long pause. Then Aimee said, "You know, I've been looking at this girl in St. Petersburg who has skills similar to yours. Perhaps I should give her an audition to work for me by seeing if *she* can acquire the item from Janvier."

"We're not to that point yet," Erica snapped. "I'll let you know when we are, but it's not now. And where do you get off looking for someone to replace me? Me? After all we've bene through?"

"We have been through a lot, and you've always come through, but you're not yourself lately, and this is still a business." Aimee paused for a minute. "Very well. I'll give you eight weeks to acquire the item. Then I'm going to reassign you and bring the Russian in to see what she can do. Understood?"

"I understand."

Aimee ended the call. Erica stared at her phone. She looked at the time and realized that it was after ten in the morning. She sent Josh a quick text. *"What time do you want me at your hotel tonight, and where do you want to go?"*

Josh texted back, *"Gambling, and six o'clock."*

Erica replied, *"Sounds like fun. I'll be there with a change of clothes at six."*

Josh texted back, *"Don't forget the clothes you want to wear tomorrow night and Sunday."*

"Will do," Erica shut down her computer and went to bed.

CHAPTER 7

Erica arrived at Josh's hotel at ten minutes before six that evening. She had her overnight bag with her. She took the elevator up to Josh's floor and knocked on his door.

When the door opened, Josh smiled and motioned for her to come inside. Once the door was closed, and Erica had put the overnight bag on the floor, they wrapped their arms around each other and started kissing each other passionately.

"I've... missed you... this week," Josh said, kissing her.

"I missed... you, too..." Erica responded. "I... can't... make love... to a... text... message."

After several minutes, Erica pulled away and said, "If we keep doing this, we're going to have to move to the bedroom, and then we won't get any dinner. I don't know about you, but I'm starving."

She didn't mention that the reason she was so hungry is that she'd missed breakfast because she was trying to find a way to break into Janvier's house, and she missed lunch because she was sleeping.

Josh grinned. "Fine. Plenty of time for the bedroom after we get back. Shall we go?"

Erica nodded. Josh grabbed his coat, and they went downstairs to catch a cab.

"Where do you want to eat?" Erica asked as they waited for the cab.

"How about at the casino?" Josh suggested. "I hear the restaurant is pretty good."

Erica smiled. "I like that idea."

A cab pulled up to the hotel entrance. Josh gave the driver the address of the casino, and soon they were heading east through Paris.

They arrived at the casino thirty minutes later and headed for the restaurant. After being seated, Josh ordered a steak, and Erica order the salmon. Both meals were excellent.

After dinner, they exchanged euros for chips at the cashier's cage, and then they headed for the Poker 21 tables. Erica didn't do too badly, but Josh was the big winner at their table. When the Croupier changed the decks the second time, though, Josh's luck began to wane.

Josh and Erica moved to the *Punto Banco* tables, where they played the Parisian version of Baccarat for several hours. They both did well, and shortly before midnight, she suggested checking out the Texas Hold 'Em tables.

They found a table with two empty seats and began playing. As with the two other times they'd played against each other, Erica did much better, cleaning out most of the other players. Josh increased the number of chips in front of him, but he didn't do anywhere near as well as Erica.

On the last hand they played at the table, Josh folded quickly, but Erica kept playing until four of the players had gone all-in. She pushed her chips into the pot, and when the players had to show their cards, Erica had the high hand, winning the largest pot so far.

Erica and Josh decided it was time to call it a night, so they walked to the cashier's cage and had their winnings transferred to their bank accounts.

"What will you do with your winnings?" Josh asked, once

they were in the cab heading back to his hotel.

"I don't know," Erica replied. "I'm thinking of retiring, so I'll probably use it to start a new life somewhere warm."

"Are you serious?" Josh asked.

Erica nodded. "My boss has already started looking at someone to replace me, so it feels like it's time to walk away. My assignment with The Janvier Group will probably be my last. I want a life, not just a career, and I don't think I can have both. It's time to get out on my own terms and see if I can start enjoying all the things I've been missing."

"I've been thinking along the same lines," Josh said. "I know I'm being considered for Partner, but if I take that job, I'll never have a life at all. I've been thinking about going home. I haven't been there in over ten years. I've got enough money stashed away to live well, while doing something that keeps me from getting bored. There probably won't be a better time to get out of the game."

"Where do you see *us* in that plan?" Erica asked.

Josh looked at her. "We haven't really discussed the future of *us*, but if we're both thinking of leaving our current jobs and having a life for a change, it opens a lot of possibilities. I don't know exactly what I'd do if I did walk away from my career, but I'd love to do it with you."

"I'd love that, too," Erica admitted. "What's a life without someone to share it with?"

"Exactly."

She stifled a yawn and snuggled up next to Josh as they rode to his hotel.

When they arrived, they went up to Josh's room. "I imagine you're too tired to do anything but sleep," Josh said.

Erica nodded. "I'm sorry, but it was a long day. I promise I'll make it up to you tomorrow."

"No worries," Josh said pleasantly. "Just having you here with me is all I need to be happy."

Erica's eyes twinkled mischievously. "Then what I have planned for tomorrow should make you ecstatic."

"I'll hold you to that."

They undressed and put their clothes away. Josh pulled on a pair of sleep shorts, and Erica put on an oversized t-shirt. They crawled into bed, and Erica moved as close to him as she could. "I love you," she said softly.

Josh kissed her neck. "I love you."

Erica woke up and looked at the clock on Josh's nightstand. It was five-thirty in the morning. She had been asleep for only three-and-a-half hours, but she was wide-awake. She turned and looked at Josh, who was sleeping deeply next to her.

He is a seriously handsome man, she thought. *And right now I want him more than I've ever wanted a man before. Do I wake him, or do I wait until he wakes up on his own?*

Erica tried to go back to sleep, but at six o'clock, she was still wide-awake and becoming more frustrated by the minute. Finally, she reached down so she could pleasure herself.

As her fingers reached for her pleasure centers, so she could release the sexual tension that had been building up, she felt Josh's hand pull hers out of the way.

"I think that's my job," he whispered.

She felt a part of him growing and pressing against her thigh. She turned so he could reach her more easily, and she slipped her hand into his shorts and began helping that part of him grow even more. As her hand moved up and down on him, and as his fingers worked their magic on her, she cried out as she climaxed. Once the sensation finally subsided, she removed her shirt and rolled over into her knees. She threw the covers back, removed Josh's shorts, and moved on top of him.

Josh penetrated her immediately, and Erica moaned loudly

as she felt stimulated to her very core. She climaxed again, trembling as the rolling waves of pleasure took control of her.

Josh broke the connection and slid out from under her. He got on his knees behind her, causing Erica's legs to twitch as he immediately hit one of her pleasure spots. She climaxed shortly after that, and Josh had to hold onto her waist to keep her from collapsing flat on the bed and breaking the connection.

When she was finally able to stop trembling, Josh rolled her onto her back. She wrapped her long legs around him, crossing her ankles so she could keep the connection as close as possible. She climaxed again, and Josh felt himself at the point of release. When he did, Erica cried out in delight as she felt his warmth deep inside. She hugged Josh tightly, keeping her ankles crossed. She kissed him repeatedly, letting her actions demonstrate how much she loved him.

When she finally released him, he lay next to her, and she turned to face him, placing one arm across his chest and one leg between his.

"Good morning," she said finally.

"Yes, it is," Josh agreed. "Sorry you had to start without me."

"That's okay," she purred. "You caught up nicely."

"Happy New Year's Eve," he said, nuzzling her neck.

"Same to you. Are you hungry?"

"I will be, once I catch my breath," Josh said.

"We're gonna have to work on your stamina if we're going to build a life together," Erica joked. She knew he could last as long as she could in bed. He had proven that Christmas night.

"I think my stamina is perfectly able to keep up with yours," Josh retorted. "But remember, I just woke up."

Erica felt movement against her thigh again. "And it seems some parts of you are more awake than others."

"It's a guy thing," Josh said, grinning. "I can't do a thing about it."

"I can."

Erica moved on top of him again and slowly moved down until her lips found what they wanted. Josh moaned as he ran his fingers through her hair, letting her tongue send shockwaves of pleasure through him.

After several minutes, he said, "Spin around."

Without breaking the connection, she spun around so he could pleasure her at the same time. Soon she was climaxing, but her lips and tongue continued working their magic. When Josh felt the release building, he let her know, but she continued without stopping. He released, and the stimulation from her tongue kept him releasing uncontrollably.

When she finally broke the connection, she said, "Damn, Josh. That was impressive."

"So were you," he said, rubbing his hands gently along her hips and lower back.

Erica spun around so her head was on his shoulder. "I'll never question your stamina again."

They showered, and then they ordered room service for breakfast. They spent the rest of the day watching American holiday movies on television—dubbed into French, which caused them to laugh at the bad translations.

At nine that evening, after finishing dinner from room service, which included two bottles of champagne for them to take with them, they decided to head out to the *Champs-Elysées* to participate in the New Year's Eve festivities.

The cab let them out near the Louvre, since the *Champs-Elysées* was blocked to traffic from the Louvre all the way to the Arc de Triomphe, where the fireworks display would occur at midnight. The musical performances were set to begin at ten o'clock that night, and both Erica and Josh wanted to arrive well before those started.

Erica had the bottles of champagne in the large bag slung over her shoulder. They had decided to forgo glasses, preferring to drink from the bottles instead.

"Welcome to *La Réveillon de Saint Sylvestre*," Erica said. "That's what the French call New Year's Eve."

"It's quite a sight," Josh said. "I'm glad I'm here with you."

Food vendors all along the avenue were selling both savory and sweet delectables, and Erica and Josh indulged themselves on the sweets. They walked the length of the *Champs-Elysées* hand-in-hand, enjoying being in Paris and in love. In that moment, nothing else mattered in the world.

The crowds grew steadily, but everyone seemed determined to have a good time. Josh and Erica could hear the musical acts, but neither of them ever found where the acts were set up along the avenue. There were too many people milling around.

Around eleven-thirty, Erica pulled out the bottles of champagne. "Thirsty?" she asked.

Josh nodded and took one of the bottles from her. He removed the foil and wire and then carefully popped the cork. Erica did the same, and soon they were toasting each other and drinking from their own bottles.

Erica felt the familiar sensation that champagne caused in her. She felt uninhibited, and the more she drank, the more aroused she became. Fortunately, most of the crowd was participating in public displays of affection, so no one seemed to notice that Erica couldn't stop making out with Josh.

When the countdown to midnight began, and the crowd began chanting "*Dix... neuf... huit...*" Josh and Erica downed the last of the champagne, tossed the bottles into a nearby trashcan, and hugged each other, staring deeply into each other's eyes. When the countdown reached one, and the fireworks and light show started, Erica's lips found Josh's, and they kissed in the New Year while the Parisians and tourists around them danced, sang, and cheered, welcoming the first moments of January.

Once the fireworks were finished, they headed to one of the nearby streets where traffic was still open so they could catch a cab back to Josh's hotel. It took nearly thirty minutes to find one, but eventually they were heading west to La Defense.

When they arrived at the hotel, they headed up to the room. As soon as Josh opened the door, Erica began undressing. Josh did the same. When he looked up, Erica was standing in the window, her lean, tanned body silhouetted by the lights from the La Defense business district.

He moved toward her, and she threw her arms around him. They kissed, and she reached down, feeling him stiffen and grow in her hand. He reached down and began pleasuring her as well. After a few minutes, Erica turned around and leaned forward, placing her hands on the window. Josh held her hips in his hands as he thrust.

Erica began moaning unrestrained as the intensity increased. Josh used his hands to stimulate her with his fingers at the same time. Erica trembled as the sensations felt like electricity coursing through her body. Her skin glistened with sweat.

As the first climax subsided, she turned around and pushed Josh into the bedroom and onto the bed. Her lips and tongue took over, causing Josh's legs to tremble. After several minutes of mind-numbing stimulation—just when Josh didn't think he could last another minute—Erica moved on top of him.

She moaned and her breathing became deeper as her stomach muscles spasmed and her legs shook uncontrollably. Erica cried out in pleasure, wanting the climaxes to end and wishing they wouldn't in equal measure.

Josh felt his own release building. Both of them were bathed in sweat by this time, but neither seemed to notice.

Erica cried out as the next climax hit her. This one was so intense that she nearly lost consciousness. But the sensations kept her in the moment, and she clutched the sheets to have something to hold onto and keep her tethered to this world as she felt herself approaching a level of ecstasy she had never felt before.

She could tell that Josh was about to release, but all she wanted was for him to continue. "Don't stop," she cried out over and over. She felt his release, but he didn't stop. A moment later, she felt herself crash through a new threshold in pleasure and began thrashing as her muscles stopped obeying her and began spasming and trembling beyond anything she had ever experienced. She no longer knew who or where she was. All she knew is that Josh was with her, making her feel things she didn't know were possible.

Before she knew it, she was crying. She didn't know why, but she couldn't stop. Josh broke the connection and just held her until the tears stopped. He grabbed the box of tissues on the nightstand and put the box next to her.

"Are you all right?" he asked gently as she wiped her eyes.

She nodded, unable to speak. Josh got them both bottles of water from the fridge in the other room. After they had drunk, Josh asked, "What was that?"

"Heaven," Erica responded. "I don't know what else to call it. It was like nothing I've felt before. At one point I thought I was going to pass out, and at another point I thought I had died and was trapped inside an endless orgasm. If you could bottle and sell what you did to me, you'd be the richest man alive."

"I love you, Erica. After you're rested, we'll have to see if we can do it again."

"I love you, Josh, but that may have to wait until next weekend," Erica said, taking another swig of water. "I'm not sure I'm capable of feeling anything right now."

Josh pulled up the covers and held Erica until they both fell asleep.

Josh and Erica spent most of New Year's Day together, but after an early dinner in Josh's room, Erica reluctantly left to return to her own hotel. The next day was her first day working with The Janvier Group, and she needed to be prepared. Not only did she have a legitimate assignment to evaluate Janvier's office real estate holdings and plans, but she still had an object that she was being paid to recover for her client. She needed time to prepare to do both.

The next morning, Erica arrived at The Carpe Diem building and was escorted to the security office on the twenty-seventh floor. Günter Reinhardt, the head of Security, provided Erica with the credentials she would need to access all of the company's offices in France. Then he escorted her upstairs for her meeting with Étienne Laurent, who was overseeing her work.

Josh saw her walk past his office. She turned and waved on her way to Laurent's office. Josh smiled and then returned to his work, which had been piling up on his desk.

Erica spent the next three days touring the offices around Paris. She returned to The Carpe Diem building on Thursday so she could arrange tours of the offices outside the city.

Late Thursday afternoon, Laurent stopped by her office on his way out. "How's everything going?"

"Fine, sir," she replied. "I have tours scheduled next week for the other offices, and each office manager has promised to provide floorplans, copies of leases, and occupancy information by the end of next week."

"Wonderful," Laurent said. "Well, I have a management meeting to get to. Let me know if you need anything."

"You're meeting with Mr. Janvier?" Erica asked. "I like to meet him one of these days."

Laurent nodded. "It's an off-site meeting, and everyone else left thirty minutes ago. I'll be late, as always. We'll talk more tomorrow. Good night."

"Good night, sir."

Erica watched him head for the elevators. *Janvier and the senior managers are out of the office tonight. It might be a good time to search his office. Good thing I brought my kit with me.*

Erica waited until the cleaning crew was finished with her floor. She had learned from the office manager that the cleaning crew always started on the top floor and worked their way down. Erica knew that she shouldn't bump into any of the cleaning staff or her co-workers on her floor or on Janvier's floor.

She took her kit—hidden in her drawstring bag—to the restroom down the hall. She changed into the black unitard and other clothing she wore when she broke into the interior design company, renovation contractor, and security company that had updated Janvier's residence. She also pulled on a safety harness to protect her while climbing up to next floor where Janvier's office was located.

At the far end of the restroom, there was a small closet containing cleaning supplies and paper products. Next to that was a large air vent that connected to the smaller of the two airshafts running from the basement to the top floor.

Erica hid her bag in the closet and opened the mesh vent cover. She stuck her head inside the airshaft, looking for the best way to move between floors. On the wall of the airshaft, about four feet from the vent, was a metal rung ladder that ran the full length of the shaft.

Erica looked down and saw that there were no ledges anywhere in the airshaft. Apart from the ladder rungs, there was nothing between her and the basement floor below. The metal walls of the airshaft were smooth, and she could hear the sound of the forced air system delivering warm air to all of the floors in the building.

Erica removed a large device with two industrial suction cups on each end. She placed it on the inside wall of the airshaft just above the vent. After securing the suction cups, she tested the device to make certain that it was properly stuck to the wall. Then she attached a rope to the device. She hooked the other end of the first rope to the safety harness she was wearing. She took a second length of rope and swung it toward the ladder rungs. After two tries, the metal catch caught one of the rungs and locked. Erica attached the other end of the second rope to her harness.

She swung herself into the airshaft and closed the vent grate. The suction cup device held her up. She pulled herself over to the ladder rungs with the second rope. Once she was standing on the rungs, she disconnected the first rope from her harness—connected to the suction cup device—and attached the free end to one of the rungs, leaving it ready for her return. Then she disconnected the second rope from the ladder rung and climbed up to the next floor.

When she reached the thirty-first floor, she attached the metal catch at the end of the second rope to the closest ladder rung. Getting from the ladder to the air vent proved to be more of a challenge than getting from the air vent to the ladder. She attached a suction cup device to each hand, and reaching as far as she could, she attached one of the suction cups to the wall. She let go of the ladder rungs and swung so her weight was being held up by the one suction cup. She attached the suction cup in her other hand to the wall, released the first suction cup, and reached as far as she could before reattaching that suction cup to the wall.

She did this several times until she had reached the vent cover. After looking through the grate to make certain that the restroom was empty, she pushed the vent grate open and swung her legs through. She detached the second rope from her belt and looped it through the two suctions cups.

Erica crossed the restroom to the door. She cracked it open and listened. She heard no voices or movement. She slipped through the door, looking around for security cameras. Finding none, she proceeded to Janvier's office.

The outer office was empty, and there were no lights coming from the office. Erica slipped into his office, surprised that the door was not locked. She walked around the edge of the office until she reached the hallway behind the bookcase leading to his apartment.

Not seeing any cameras in the apartment, she began searching for the object she had been tasked with recovering. After nearly an hour, she concluded that the item was not in the apartment. *At least I can finally rule out the apartment and start concentrating all my effort on Janvier's house.*

She quickly made her way back to the restroom and reattached the second rope to her safety harness. Using one of the suction cups, she swung herself through the vent grate and closed it behind her. Then she released the suction cup and swung on the second rope to the ladder rungs. She climbed down to the thirtieth floor and reattached her safety harness to the first rope, connected to the suction cup device over the vent grate.

She looped the second rope through one of the ladder rungs and hooked it to her safety harness. Now the second rope from the ladder was attached at both ends to her belt. If the suction cup device failed to support her weight, the second rope looped through the ladder rung would still keep her from falling.

She tested the first rope, attached to the suction cup device, to make certain that it was still secure, and she allowed herself to swing from the ladder until she was directly below the vent grate. She climbed up, pushed open the vent grate, grabbed the bottom edge of the vent, and pulled herself back into the restroom. She unhooked one end of the second rope from her safety belt and pulled it loose from the ladder. She then disconnected the suction cup device from above the vent.

She retrieved her bag, changed clothes, and put her tools and break-in outfit into the bag. Then she returned to her office to pack up her briefcase and head back to her hotel for the night.

All-in-all, it had been a successful break-in, even though the object she was looking for was not there.

Laurent arrived at Janvier's home ten minutes late. He parked on the street and strode quickly to the front door. Once inside, one of the guards said, "You're late. The rest are upstairs."

"I know," Laurent said, removing his coat and hanging it in the coatroom.

The security guard took Laurent's keys to park his car in the parking deck nearby, while another guard escorted Laurent up to the fifth floor where Janvier's home theatre was located.

Laurent entered the theatre. One of his colleagues from another business was giving his report. Laurent bowed to Janvier, and took his seat. Janvier acknowledged Laurent, but said nothing. Laurent removed his notebook and pen, put his briefcase on the floor next to him, and looked around the room.

The room was filled with the key executives from all of Janvier's businesses—legitimate and otherwise. Four of the people in the room were part of The Janvier Group—Janvier's legitimates businesses—but the other fifteen people, apart from Raphaël Janvier himself, were from Janvier's illegal businesses.

The man speaking was the head of Janvier's illegal arms smuggling business. Normally, Laurent wouldn't be concerned with Janvier's illegal businesses, but lately, the illegal businesses were taking advantage of Laurent's operating divisions to launder money and serve as front companies for illegal activities. Against all expectations—and against his wishes—Laurent was seeing more and more overlaps between The Janvier Group's legitimate enterprises and Janvier's illegal operations, something that would never have been allowed a year earlier.

"Are there any questions?" Janvier asked when the head of

arms smuggling was finished speaking.

Laurent stood. "I apologize for being late, Raphaël, and if this was covered already, please excuse the redundancy. Last month, The Janvier Group's shipping subsidiary was asked to transport three shipping containers from Sicily to central Africa on behalf of the previous speaker. The month before, three other shipping containers were transported to and from the same ports on behalf of the previous speaker. In the past, we have tried to keep The Janvier Group independent from your other businesses, but this seems to have changed in the past year. There are numerous overlaps, including the comingling of funds through your legitimate businesses and using subsidiaries of The Janvier Group as front companies for smuggling, trafficking, arms sales, money laundering, and the like. Were these overlaps just business events born of urgent necessity, or are the lines between your businesses blurring so that we'll be seeing more activities like this in the coming years?" Laurent took his seat.

Janvier nodded. "I was going to cover that a little later in greater detail, but the simple answer to your question is: Yes, we will be seeing more activities like this in the coming years. Does this pose a problem for you, Étienne?"

Laurent shook his head. "No, sir. My concern has to do with the operational-improvement study that's underway. We have a consultant currently examining all of our operations so he can make recommendations related to our acquisition strategies. There is a very real possibility that he might discover these overlaps, which would be very unfortunate. And even if he doesn't discover them, there's the real possibility that his recommendations might interfere with the way these overlaps are currently structured, causing us to have to redefine how the overlaps will work in light of the redesigned operational models. I recommend that we limit these overlaps as much as possible until the current operational study is concluded next month, and then proceed cautiously as those recommendations are being implemented."

Janvier rocked on his heels and stroked his chin. "I hadn't considered that. Unfortunately, these overlaps are necessary and cannot be limited, but we can limit any new overlaps as you suggested. In the meantime, keep a close watch on the consultant who's performing the study. If he discovers the overlaps, report that to me immediately. We can't afford to have an outsider stumble upon something that could invite investigations from law enforcement."

"And what will you do if he does discover the overlaps?" Laurent asked.

"The same thing that happens to anyone who could potentially interfere in my business," Janvier stated.

Laurent nodded. *In other words, Josh will disappear into a deep and watery grave. I'd hate for that to happen to him. Hopefully, he won't find anything that will require me to notify Raphaël. I have no interest in causing the death of an innocent contractor who was just doing his job.*

Security guards entered the theatre and set up serving tables. They brought in a variety of cold and hot foods in buffet-style serving containers. Once everyone had filled their plates and returned to their seats, the meeting continued.

It was well after midnight when the meeting finally ended. Laurent was deeply disturbed by the plans Raphaël had for involving The Janvier Group more and more in the illegal activities of his other businesses. Laurent felt trapped. *I don't want our legitimate businesses potentially coming under investigation for illegal activities, but I can't leave the company now that I know what I know. I'd be considered a liability, and I'd find myself in a deep watery grave… along with my family. I have no choice but to make it work, but at least I can do my best to keep the infected business units far away from our legitimate enterprises, so if they have to be jettisoned to protect the rest of the company, it can be done quickly and easily.*

Janvier walked up to Laurent. "Étienne, can you come into my office for a minute?"

"Of course, Raphaël."

Laurent followed Janvier up to the sixth floor. As they walked through Janvier's art gallery, he noticed two new pieces. "I see you've acquired some new items."

Janvier turned and smiled. "Yes, I have." He pointed to a freestanding display case with a beautiful jewel encrusted peacock. "This is the 'Van der Waal Peacock' by the renowned artist Horst Van der Waal. It's worth thirty million euros."

Janvier then pointed to the front wall between the two windows overlooking the front yard and the street. "And this magnificent masterpiece is Rembrandt's 'The Storm on the Sea of Galilee'."

Laurent stood, admiring Janvier's latest acquisitions. He had worked with Janvier long enough to know that every piece of art in this gallery and the gallery on the other side of the central staircase was stolen. Glancing around the room, he saw other masterpieces that Janvier had acquired illegally, including Van Gogh's "Poppy Flowers," Picasso's "Le Pigeon aux Petits Pois," and Monet's "Charing Cross Bridge, London" which was thought to have been destroyed, but which Janvier had acquired from the original thieves before they destroyed the other paintings they had stolen in the same robbery. Laurent estimated that Janvier was in possession of well over a billion euro's worth of priceless, stolen, works of art.

Janvier motioned for Laurent to follow him to the office at the far end of the gallery. When they entered the office, Laurent saw a stack of envelopes on the corner of the desk.

"I wanted to give you the gala invitations for the key staff at The Janvier Group," Janvier explained, handing the stack to Laurent. "Will you handle distributing them in person for me?"

"I'd be delighted, Raphaël." Laurent looked through the envelopes to see who had earned an invitation to this year's

Valentine's Day gala. When he reached the bottom of the stack, he saw Josh's name.

"Josh MacGregor is getting an invitation?"

Janvier nodded. "I've read his preliminary report and recommendations that you forwarded to me, and if we implement even half of what he's suggesting, he'll be responsible for contributing more to our bottom line—in terms of cost savings and expansion capabilities—than any single person I've ever employed. I'd say that deserves an invitation, don't you?"

"Certainly, Raphaël," Laurent agreed. "It'll be interesting to see who he brings as his plus-one."

"If he doesn't have someone to bring, offer to make arrangements with one of the finer establishments in Paris for companionship that evening. My treat. We can't have him attend a Valentine's Day gala solo."

"I'll take care of it," Laurent said.

Janvier nodded. "I'll walk you downstairs, Étienne."

"That's not necessary, Raphaël. I know the way. Have a good night, and I'll see you in the office next week."

"Good night, then, Étienne."

Laurent placed the invitations into his briefcase and walked down to the main floor to collect his coat. One of the security guards had already brought his car around. He climbed inside and drove home.

When Erica returned to her hotel, she called Aimee.

"The item is not in Janvier's apartment. If he still has it, it must be in his house."

"How are you going to get it?" Aimee asked.

"I don't know. I'm still working on it."

"Work faster."

"I know how much time you gave me," Erica snapped, "and if I can't get it done by then, I'll let you replace me. But not before then."

"Fine. Keep me posted."

Erica ended the call. *Retirement is really beginning to sound like a good idea. I'm getting too old to be swinging on ropes in air shafts, and I'm too tired of never being able to have a normal life. Aimee becoming more and more unreasonable isn't helping things.*

Erica wondered if Josh was the reason she was no longer satisfied with her career choices. *No, I was already getting frustrated... I just never let myself think about it or considered that I had options. Josh just opened my eyes to what I could have. Before, retirement meant just running away from my life. Now, thanks to Josh, I have something to run towards... assuming I don't blow it.*

Erica ordered room service for dinner and put away her break-in gear.

Étienne Laurent called Josh into his office on Friday morning.

"What do you need, Étienne?" Josh asked when he took a seat across from Laurent's desk.

"Raphaël wanted me to give you this," Laurent said, sliding an envelope across the table.

"What's this?" Josh asked, picking up the envelope.

"An invitation," Laurent replied. "Every Valentine's Day, Raphaël hosts a very large winter gala at his home. He has extended an invitation to you for this year's event—traditional black tie. You'll need to present the invitation to enter his home, and the invitation includes you and a plus-one, so you're to bring a date. If you don't have someone to bring, I've been authorized to make arrangements for someone to be your date for the evening."

Josh looked at the invitation, which had beautifully calligraphy done with gold ink on deep red cardstock. "Thank you for this, and please tell Mr. Janvier that I'm honored to be invited and I look forward to attending."

"Shall I make arrangements for your plus-one?" Laurent asked.

"That's not necessary, thank you," Josh replied. "As it happens, I do have someone I can bring."

Laurent smiled. "Very well. I'll inform Jenevieve that you have R.S.V.P.'d."

Josh nodded and left the office. He knew that Erica was supposed to be working in the building that morning, so he walked to her office. She was so busy reading what looked like a real-estate contract that she didn't see him enter the office and sit down across from her.

After a couple of minutes, he cleared his throat. She looked up, startled, but when she saw it was Josh, she grinned.

"It's not nice to sneak up on people," she said.

"I honestly thought you knew I was sitting here and decided to ignore me anyway," Josh responded.

"I'd never do that," she purred.

Josh nodded. "I hope not. Change of subject. Do you have plans for Valentine's Day?"

Erica cocked her head. "That's a long way off. I don't know what I'll be doing in two weeks, let alone six weeks. Why?"

Josh held up the invitation. "I've been invited to the Valentine's gala at Raphaël Janvier's home, and I'm inviting you to be my plus-one. Interested?"

Erica stared at Josh open-mouthed. "Interested? You bet I'm interested! What kind of party is it?"

"Traditional formal. Black ties and evening dresses."

"Can I get away with wearing the same dress I wore on Christmas Eve?" Erica asked.

"Why not? I'll be wearing the same tux."

Erica laughed. "Yes, but it's different for women. No one besides you saw me in that dress, though, so it's not like anyone would know that I only have one formal dress with me. And dark red should work for a Valentine's event, don't you think?"

"I think you look stunning in that dress," Josh replied. You already know I love how you look in it, and I think you'll turn every head there."

Erica beamed. "Then it's a date! Thanks for inviting me."

"Thanks for being available. Are you coming over tonight?"

Erica nodded and pointed to her overnight bag on the floor next to her coat rack. "Can we take the shuttle to your hotel together?"

"Absolutely. Call me when you're ready to leave."

"I will."

Josh got up, blew her a kiss, and walked back to his office.

Erica was elated. *I knew I'd never get inside Janvier's house without an invitation, and now I have an invitation! I need to let Aimee know.*

She closed her office door, took out her cell phone, and dialed Aimee's number. When Aimee answered, Erica said in a very quiet voice, "I have good news."

"Tell me."

"Janvier has a gala at his home on Valentine's Day. I've been invited. Now, I have a way in."

"That's great!" Aimee said. "How did you manage an invitation?"

"Josh is taking me as his plus-one."

"The guy who helped you get the job at The Janvier Group? You're still interacting with him?"

"Hey, he's my way in," Erica reminded Aimee. "I don't

discard anyone who can help me until the job is done. You know that."

"I'd tell you to be careful, but I'm too happy with how things are working out. Are you planning to just reconnoiter that night, or are you planning to attempt the recovery of the item?"

"I think I need to be prepared for any opportunity," Erica replied.

"And how will you explain that to Josh if you decide to recover the item?"

"I'll figure that out when and if it happens."

"Okay. You know what you're doing, and you've certainly been lucky with his help, so do what you think is best. I'll make arrangements to be in Paris that night, just in case you do recover the item. It'll probably be best if it's not with you or in Paris once it's discovered missing."

"Good plan. That way you can deliver it to the client, and I can disappear. If anyone does find me, the item won't be on me, so there'll be no proof that I took it."

"Knowing that you could be freed up in February, I'll start looking at new clients who don't mind waiting until then."

Erica hesitated for a moment. "We need to talk before that happens."

"What do you mean?" Aimee demanded. "There are clients who have waited months for you to be available. Why make them wait any longer?"

"Because I'm not sure when or if I'll be available after this caper."

"Because you want a vacation? Fine. Take a couple of weeks to get refreshed, and we'll start the next assignment in March."

"No. I don't need a vacation. I... I want out," Erica stated.
"WHAT?!"

"You heard me," Erica said.

"No, I didn't. And even if I did, I didn't. We need to talk

about this. You can't make a rushed decision like this and then just drop it on me."

"Why not? You've already been looking at my replacement, or is the Russian you told me about just a hollow threat to get me to work harder and faster?"

There was a long pause. Then Aimee said, "Look, bringing in the Russian is just so we can take on more clients, and I felt that another person could take some of the burden off of you while you get your head back in the game. It's not that I've lost faith, it's that I'm worried about you. Look, don't make any final decisions right now. Focus on Janvier, and we'll talk about this once you've recovered the item, okay?"

"Fine, but don't think you're going to change my mind," Erica said. "This has been building for a while, I've just never been able to put into words what I've been feeling. Now, I can. I want out... I need out before this job consumes me. I want a normal life, assuming I even know what normal is anymore."

"Well, we'll see," Aimee said. "Just don't make any plans until we talk."

"Fine."

Erica ended the call. *I can't believe I said that to Aimee, but now that it's said, I'm more convinced than ever that it's the right thing to do. I wonder what Josh will think when I tell him?*

Erica saw Laurent coming down the hall toward her office. *Time to get back to my other work.*

CHAPTER 8

Friday night, Josh and Erica took the company shuttle to Josh's hotel.

"How was your first week at The Janvier Group?" Josh asked.

"Very productive," Erica replied. "I've got a good feel for how the company is using its office spaces, and I'm already coming up with ideas to streamline the number of leases the company has and how to reconfigure the space to enhance efficiency."

Josh chuckled.

"What's so funny," Erica asked.

"This is the first time I've heard you talk shop. Up until now, everything we've talked about has been personal. I'm starting to see what you're like when you're working, and I'm intrigued, but it'll take some getting used to."

Erica nodded. "I get that. A lot of couples never get to see both the personal and professional sides of their significant others. You're seeing a new side of me. I hope it doesn't change your opinion of me."

"Not a chance," Josh said, pulling Erica close. "I can't think of anything that could make me love you any less."

"Just remember that you said that," Erica joked. What she

didn't say out loud was *"When you find out what my other career has been, just remember that we love each other very much, and that means forgiving… transgressions."*

Erica spent the weekend with Josh. Now that the holidays were over, and Paris was returning to normal, they spent more time exploring museums, taking day trips to some of the palaces and chateaus, ordering room service, and enjoying each other's company in the bedroom. It was as close to being a normal couple as two people could be, given that they were living in hotels because their work had taken them far from their homes.

Erica loved being in a normal relationship with Josh, even though it terrified her at the same time. Her biggest fear was Josh discovering her other career and the risks she was taking by being with him. Part of her still believed that she could walk away from him without any regrets, but the more time they spent together, the more Erica knew that was impossible.

Erica spent the next week meeting with real estate agencies to look at alternative office space in the Paris area, and meeting with office furniture wholesalers to see what was available for the renovation of The Janvier Group's offices. In addition to being a highly successful cat burglar, she was also a talented interior designer, which is why she used that job as her cover when approaching new targets. She didn't just talk a good game, she could actually do the work, and her design clients spoke very highly of her talents—including clients she had robbed.

Josh spent the week wrestling with a number of strange situations that he had uncovered while reviewing the operational reports provided by Laurent's people. In addition to the business units under The Janvier Group, he had discovered other businesses owned by Raphaël Janvier that shared resources, bank accounts, and inventory with The Janvier Group. In fact, at first glance, it looked like parts of The Janvier Group were being used as fronts for unlisted business activities.

At his status update with Laurent on Friday, Josh mentioned that he had found some anomalies in the business activities of several divisions. When he showed Laurent the data, Laurent dismissed Josh's concerns.

"Don't worry about the interactions between The Janvier Group and other businesses owned by Mr. Janvier. He tries to keep his various businesses separate, but there are times when it's advantageous for there to be some… overlaps."

"These overlaps seem quite substantial—"

"And from time to time that might be true," Laurent interrupted. "But it is sporadic at best. Any interactions between Mr. Janvier's businesses that are not part of The Janvier Group specifically are to be ignored, okay? Mr. Janvier will continue using his businesses as he sees fit. Your job is to help The Janvier Group operate as a single company so we can renew our acquisition strategies and continue our rapid growth."

Laurent's tone told Josh that the discussion was over. "Very well," Josh said. "Thank you for clarifying the situation."

Josh stood to leave, but Laurent said, "By the way, your recommendation of Erica Longwood's services was fantastic. She is doing a great job for us. Thank you for that."

Josh smiled and nodded, then returned to his own office.

Laurent watched Josh leave the office. *Raphaël specifically told me to watch for any signs that Josh had stumbled onto instances where his other businesses overlapped with The Janvier Group's*

operations. It was inevitable that someone with his talents might find overlaps, but do I let Raphaël know about this conversation? If I do, he might unnecessarily eliminate Josh out of an overabundance of caution. If I don't, and Josh continues digging into these overlaps, he might eliminate both of us.

Laurent drummed his fingers on his desk, deep in thought. *I'll keep an eye on Josh and make sure he's not pursuing this. If he does, then I'll tell Raphaël. If he doesn't, then there's nothing to tell.*

That night, over dinner, Erica noticed something bothering Josh. "Are you all right? You seem distracted."

Josh stared at his plate, toying with his food. Then he said, "I know we agreed not to talk about business, but do you mind if I break that rule?"

"Is it that important to you?" she asked.

Josh nodded.

"Okay, shoot. What's bothering you?"

"I stumbled onto something this week… something I don't think I was supposed to see."

"What?"

"I think I found evidence of The Janvier Group fronting for some of Janvier's other businesses."

"What other businesses?" Erica asked.

"That's just it," Josh said, putting his fork down. "I have no idea. Étienne says that these are sporadic interactions and not to worry about them, but they just don't feel… well, legal."

Erica nodded. "I've heard that he has dozens of businesses that aren't part of The Janvier Group *per se*, and there have been rumors that many of them are illegal… you know, arms dealing, smuggling, human trafficking, and the like, but nothing's ever been proven, and no legal action has ever been taken. *If* it's true, he's very good at covering his tracks. If not, then he's just another European tycoon whose reputation is larger-than-life."

"I never knew he was suspected of illegal activities," Josh said. "Why would you want a criminal as a client?"

"It's never been *proven* that he's a criminal, Josh," Erica remarked. "Besides, there's hardly a businessman as successful and ruthless as Janvier who isn't suspected of doing illegal things. It's the nature of European business dealings. So much of it is shrouded in secrecy, traditions, or the church, that intrigue is commonplace. My advice? Ignore it and focus on what you're there to do. That's what I do. If everything's legal, you don't want to waste your time chasing ghosts, and if you've found something truly illegal, then for your own safety, you need to bury that fact deep and hope Janvier's people don't suspect that you're trying to discover what's going on. That could prove very… unhealthy… for both of us, if they know we're in a relationship."

Josh nodded. "You're right. Thanks. And I don't know if they know we're a couple, but they will by Valentines when we attend the gala together. Oh, by the way, Étienne told me how pleased he is with my recommendation to bring you in. He likes the work you're doing."

Erica beamed. "That's nice to know. I'm enjoying myself there, and there's so much I can do to help them. I appreciate your recommendation."

Josh had a sly look in his eyes. "Just how much do you appreciate me for doing that?"

Erica smiled. "I'll show you when we get back to the hotel," she purred.

Josh picked up his fork and cleaned his plate in record time.

The following week, Josh and Erica were so busy that they had little time to get together. They spent the weekend together, as they usually did, but during the week, they were lucky to bump into each other at the office.

Josh finished drafting his initial findings and recommendations, being certain to leave out any references to the suspicious business dealings he had discovered. He emailed a copy to his boss and to Étienne Laurent for their review.

On the last Monday in January, Josh received an email from his boss in London. *"I'll be in Paris on Wednesday. We need to meet and review the status of your project."*

Josh replied to the email. *"I'll make myself available any time that works best for you. Just let me know when and where you want to meet."*

Josh's boss named the time and place, and Josh confirmed that he'd be there.

On Wednesday, just before noon, Josh arrived at the *Gare du Nord* Station in northern Paris' 10th *arrondissement*. This was the station used by high-speed trains between London and Paris. He walked to the *Terminus Nord* restaurant, where he was supposed to meet his boss.

Peter Olivetti, one of the Senior Partners with EPDHW Consulting LLP, was forty-eight, balding, twice divorced, and the finest consulting firm leader that Josh had ever known. When Josh first joined the firm, Peter was his mentor, teaching Josh everything a consultant needed to know to succeed in the European market. Over the years, Peter allowed Josh more and more autonomy with his client assignments, as a testament to Josh's abilities to get the job done and delight his clients. Now, Peter met with Josh in person only once a year, to review the goals for the coming year, and toward the end of each project to discuss status and next steps. This lunch was to be a combination of both.

Josh saw Peter sitting at a table in the corner. He waved and walked over.

"Hi, Peter," he said, taking a seat across the table.

"Hi, Josh. Thanks for meeting me here."

"How was the trip?" Josh asked.

"Two hours and twenty minutes of high-speed boredom," Peter responded. His detest of trains was well known in the firm.

Josh grinned. "You would have waited longer than that at the airport for a flight here," Josh reminded him.

Peter held up his hands. "I know, I know. Let's talk about the project. I read your preliminary findings and recommendations. How do you think the client will react?"

"Favorably," Josh said. "Étienne Laurent, the head of Operations, has already provided his feedback, and he forwarded a copy to Raphaël Janvier for his review and comments. Barring any unforeseen revisions, I should have the final report ready to deliver by the Friday after Valentine's Day."

Peter smiled. "And how does Laurent view you and the firm?"

"Also favorably," Josh replied. "He's already talking about *when* we begin the implementation of the recommendations."

"Perfect. I don't know if you're aware, but the partners met last week to discuss raises and promotions." Peter handed an envelope to Josh. "This is for you."

Josh opened the envelope and read the letter inside. It outlined his new salary and annual bonus, which was substantial. *More money I'll never be able to spend if I stay with the firm.* Josh read the rest of the letter, but he noticed that his job title was listed as "Pending."

"Why is my job title Pending?" he asked.

"Because your title going forward depends on what happens with The Janvier Group. If you win us the implementation contract for your recommendations, you'll be promoted to Partner. If not, you'll be promoted to Principal Senior Associate."

Josh stared at Peter. "Partner? I'm up for Partner?"

Peter nodded. "You've earned it, but the other partners want to see if you can sell Janvier on our implementation services. Partners are heavily involved in sales and managing service delivery staff, rather than actually delivering services to our clients. The other partners want to make certain that you can sell. I have no doubts, and I told them so, but I'm just one vote."

Josh was stunned. He thought he had another year to go before making partner, and he knew that the demands of being a partner meant more travel and less time for a personal life. Not a single partner with the firm had a successful marriage. Most had been divorced multiple times, including the partners who had married other partners. And the Principal Senior Associates—the highest-ranking non-partners in the firm—had a similar track record with their personal relationships. To be good at the work meant to never have a long-term meaningful relationship with anyone, and to have a successful relationship meant to be passed over for promotions on the grounds of "not being a team player."

Josh knew that, if he wanted to pursue a relationship with Erica, it would mean the end of his career; and if he wanted to pursue the partnership position, it would mean the end of his relationship with Erica.

He noticed that Peter was watching him, and Josh smiled. "Thank you, Peter. Your guidance since I joined the firm is how I got to where I am, and I'm grateful to you for everything you've done. The implementation contract should be a piece of cake to win for the firm. If you could send me the latest manpower rates, I can start working up the contract fees and let you approve the draft proposal before I submit it to Étienne Laurent."

Peter smiled and nodded like a proud father. "I have them with me." He slid a folder across the table. "I assume you'll want oversight of the project, even though—as a Partner—you won't be delivering any of the services, right?"

Josh nodded, "Unless there's something more important the

firm needs me to do."

Peter grinned. "We'll talk about that while we eat."

Peter snapped his fingers to summon the waiter—something Josh knew was an extremely rude thing to do but typical of Peter's behavior when dealing with "underlings." After they both ordered lunch, Josh asked how business was going across Europe.

"Business is booming, but competition is rising. A number of U.S.-based firms are entering the market, so we need to counter any perceived benefits those firms have over us. How would you approach that?"

Josh smiled. "If their staff is coming over from the States, they probably don't understand the nuances of doing business in the individual European countries. They'll be perceived as arrogant bullies, rather than partners. We'll always have the edge there. If their staff is being hired or acquired in Europe, then we use their inexperience working as a team over here against them. Either way, we paint them as the 'new kids,' rather than serious competition, and if they have any good staff members, we poach them."

Peter slammed his hand on the table. "And that's why you'll make an outstanding partner. You know how to operate here, and you remember what it's like to be new to this market, so you can use that knowledge and experience against other newcomers."

Josh nodded, but silently, he was laughing. *I talk a good game, and I probably would be a good partner… if I wanted to be a slave to my career until I dropped dead of a heart attack. I've only known three partners who lived long enough to retire, and even then, once retired, they had no life to enjoy. No, I plan to get out while I have my health and the promise of a life I can enjoy for years to come. But I can't let anyone know—especially not before the bonuses are paid. If they suspect I'm leaving, they'll withhold the bonus as a way to force me to stay.*

They continued chatting until their lunch arrived. After they finished eating, Peter asked, "So, what are your plans for the next few weeks?"

"I'll be finishing the final reports," Josh answered, "and there's also the annual Valentine's Day gala at Raphaël Janvier's home. He invited me to this year's soirée."

Peter's eyes bugged when he heard that. "*You* were invited? They *must* be pleased with your services. I've heard that's the hottest ticket—and the hardest to obtain—in town." Peter cocked his head to one side. "I've also heard it's couples only. Who are you going with?"

Josh smiled. "They offered to… *arrange* companionship for the evening, meaning they were going to hire someone from an escort service for me, but it turns out I actually know someone here in Paris that I'm taking."

"Are you dating someone here?"

Josh shook his head, knowing the answer that Peter was looking for. "No. Who has time for that? This is just someone who's also providing services to The Janvier Group. She's alone here, I'm alone here, so we've become friends. And when our contracts are finished, we go our separate ways. Hey, at least I didn't have to spend Christmas and New Year's alone this year."

Peter nodded. He paid the check, and then stood. "I need to catch the train back to London. Keep up the good work. You're making me very proud of you. Oh, and send me a copy of your final report and your contract proposal for the implementation services. We'll talk when you hear back from The Janvier Group."

"Will do," Josh said, shaking his boss' hand. Peter headed for the tracks, and Josh headed to the entrance so he could apologize to the waiter for Peter's behavior before catching a cab back to the office.

Marco and his men entered Janvier's home office.

"You wanted to see us, Boss?" Marco asked.

"Yes," Janvier replied. He leaned back in his high-back leather desk chair. "My annual gala is coming up on Valentines' Day. I want you and your team to handle security that night."

"We don't usually handle jobs where our faces can be seen, Boss," Marco protested. "Are you sure you want *us* handling your party?"

Janvier nodded. "It's easy work. Post someone at the back door to make sure no one enters or exits from there, post two people at the front door to check invitations and make sure no one tries to leave with any of my property, have one person in the security office watching the video monitors, and have one person standing at the foot of the stairs leading up to the sixth floor. That person can also periodically check the seventh floor, the sixth floor, and the galleries in the fifth floor to make sure nothing is missing. And—God forbid—if it snows that night, which I doubt it will, you'll all need to rotate in and out handling snow clearance from the front walk and the sidewalk where the cabs and valets will be handling the cars."

Marco looked concerned, but he simply nodded.

Janvier waved, signaling that Marco and his men were dismissed.

As they descended the stairs, one of Marco's men said, "We're to be party guards? I'd rather be out killing the competition."

Marco nodded. "Me, too. But we do what the boss wants. If he wants us to protect his home during a party, then we protect his home during a party. And he's right: It's easy work, and we get paid all the same."

Marco and his team continued down to the first floor in silence.

As the date of the gala approached, and Erica put the finishing touches on her office space utilization and interior design proposal, the weather reports began mentioning the possibility of severe weather. Temperatures dropped, forcing the vineyards in northern France to take drastic steps to protect their crops. The increased demand on the power grid in and around Paris began causing system overloads, leading to power blinks and periodic brownouts and blackouts.

Snow predictions were reported on each newscast, and as Valentine's Day grew closer, the predictions changed from a slight chance of snow, to snow with significant accumulation, to a full-on winter storm, to a potential blizzard—something not seen in Paris in many years.

The instability of the power grid—caused by increased demand for heating—gave Erica an idea. She researched the Paris power grid during other peak demand situations, and she discovered that brownouts, power blinks, and blackouts were common, since Paris had such a temperate climate that the ability to handle high demands due to extreme heat or cold was never built into the power distribution systems.

She then researched the security equipment that Janvier had installed in his house and discovered a vulnerability during constant switchovers between the electrical system and battery back-ups. The vulnerability was present in both the cameras and the laser systems.

She placed a call to Aimee. "I have a plan," she said when Aimee answered the phone.

"Hello to you, too," Aimee said. "What's your plan?"

"Have you been keeping up with the weather reports for Paris?"

"Apart from predicting snow, not really. Why?"

"It looks like we're going to get hit with either a winter

storm or a blizzard. In addition to massive snowfalls, temperatures will drop well below zero degrees Fahrenheit. When that happens, it will overload the power grid, causing blinks and blackouts. If that's happening during the gala at Janvier's house, it could give me a window of opportunity to recover the item that night. I'm going in prepared to recover it, rather than just attending the gala and using the party to reconnoiter the possibility of breaking in."

"You're going to attempt to recover the item at a gala attended by potentially hundreds of people?" Aimee sounded incredulous.

Erica chuckled. "The caper of the century, and the crowning jewel of my career. Honestly, I may never get another chance, and the weather should provide sufficient diversions to allow me to recover the item *and* get out alive. I don't think I have any choice, Aimee. This is my one shot to recover the item."

Aimee was silent. Then she said, "Okay. Do what you think is right, but how are you going to get the item out and to me with Josh there?"

"I'll figure that out when the time comes," Erica replied. "You just be here and ready to take the item back to its proper owner. And remember, the roads will be a mess."

"I'll remember," Aimee said. "What will you do after you recover the item?"

"Get out of town quickly. Make certain you wire my half of the three million euro recovery fee to my account as soon as you get it."

"Why? Where are you going to be?"

"Somewhere in the Caribbean," Erica relied.

"And what about our other assignments?" Aimee demanded.

"Give them to the Russian. After this job, I'm out. I've got money stashed away, and it's time I used it to have a life."

"Are you sure?" Aimee asked. "You and I have been doing

this since we graduated from Marymount together. We've been helping people for over ten years. That's not an easy thing to abandon. And I don't know exactly how much money you've got, but can you really afford walk away from this life? From what we've built together?"

"Actually, yes, and abandoning this career is easier than you think. I'm tired of being a thief, even if it's for the right reasons. I'm tired of risking my life every time a client calls us, I'm tired of the stress, I'm tired of living out of a suitcase in hotels, and I'm tired of Europe. I want warm weather. I want to live in the sun and sleep at night. I want to be normal."

"And just what is normal?"

"Not this," Erica replied.

"And Josh?"

Erica sighed. "Maybe he'll be part of my new normal. And maybe he won't. It's too soon to tell. But I hope he joins me."

Aimee gasped. "You *did* sleep with him, didn't you?"

"Yes, I did. More than once."

"Erica, how could you? You know that breaks your rules. You don't sleep with targets to recover items, and you don't sleep with anyone connected to a target to gain entry or access to an item being recovered. You call it your, 'I-don't-whore-myself-out-for-a-job' rule. You've only broken it once, and you remember how that turned out."

"I remember, but the heart wants what the heart wants. I'm in love, Aimee, and so is Josh. I want him, and to have him, I have to leave *Le Chat Rusé* behind me and walk away from this life. It's a price I'm willing to pay."

Aimee sighed. "Oh, girl, I always knew I might lose you one day, given the risks you take, but I never thought I'd lose you to a man you met on an assignment." She paused. "You know, if it doesn't work out with Josh, you'll always be welcome back here."

"I know. And thank you for that. But there are more Josh's

out there if things don't work out with this one. Don't count on me coming back."

"I hear you," Aimee said. "But the offer stands. No expiration date."

"Thanks, Aimee. Text me when you get to Paris."

"I will. Bye."

Erica ended the call. *No, I won't be coming back to this life ever again. I just hope I can convince Josh to come with me.*

The weekend before the gala, Erica stayed with Josh at his hotel. The snow had started falling, so they stayed inside that weekend and ordered room service.

On Sunday morning, Erica snuggled close to Josh. "Have you decided what you're going to do when your project is over?" she asked.

"I'm definitely turning down the promotion," Josh said, "which means I'll probably have to leave the firm. Turning down promotions is a career-ender. What I'll do after that is anyone's guess. I know I want to leave Europe, but where I'll go and what I'll do is up in the air. I have enough in the bank to retire on, but I feel like I'm too young to just play golf every day for the rest of my life."

"I told my business partner that I'm leaving my company, too," Erica said. "I'm tired of being a nomad, living out of suitcases and hotels. I want to go somewhere warm and tropical and never worry about demanding clients and unreasonable bosses ever again."

"I know what you mean," Josh said. "I used to be okay with the life, but not anymore. Not since I met you. I always knew that I was growing unhappy with the life, but you helped me see that there's something more important than making partner. If it weren't for you, I'd probably take the promotion and die all alone. For the first time, I feel like I actually have a chance for happiness in my life. I don't know what comes next, but I want it to be with you… if that's what you want, too."

Erica shifted so she could look at him. "That's what I want to talk to you about. I've been thinking the same things. You showed me that I could have a life—a real life—and now that's all I want. But I don't want a life without you in it. Since you don't have plans, and I don't have plans, let's make plans together. I don't want to live without you. I have a lot in the bank, and I bet you do, too. We should have more than enough to live on together and do whatever we want, wherever we want to do it. What do you think about that?"

"I think it's a great idea," Josh replied. "I don't want a life without you in it, either. Any ideas on where to begin?"

"Somewhere tropical—the Caribbean—for starters. I want to thaw out and get some sun. We can plan our future while sitting on the beach and drinking from coconuts with little umbrellas in them."

"That sounds nice," Josh agreed. "Somewhere with no bosses, no clocks, no clients, no deadlines, no offices, and no responsibilities. Just the two of us together doing whatever we want to do, when we want to do it, and as many times as we want to do it."

"You mean like what we did last night?" Erica purred.

Josh laughed. "Yes, there's that, but it doesn't have to be just that… unless that's all you want to do until we get everything else figured out."

Erica snuggled close again. "We might make time for… other things, if we want. Anything that involves you is fine with me."

"Same here," Josh said.

"So, it's settled? We run off together to an island in the Caribbean, thaw out, make love until we can barely walk, and figure out what we want to do together for the rest of our lives?"

Josh nodded. "I'm game. Now, we just need to decide which island."

"There are a lot to choose from, aren't there?" Erica noted. "The Bahamas, the Virgin Islands, Barbados, Grand Cayman, Martinique, St. Lucia, Antigua, St. Martin, St. Kitts and Nevis, Trinidad and Tobago, Turks and Caicos, plus a few others here and there."

"I've always heard that Antigua is a wonderful place," Josh said.

"Antigua it is!"

Josh leaned over and kissed her forehead. Then he said, "But what if we get to Antigua and then can't decide on what to do next?"

Erica laughed. "Josh, you decided to leave your career to be with me, and I decided to leave my career to be with you. I'm pretty sure we can both compromise and find something that we both want to do after we're done with Antigua."

Josh chuckled. "You're right."

CHAPTER 9

On the day of the party, snow blanketed the city, and more fell every hour. But the roads were clear—for the most part—and Janvier decided that the party would not be cancelled.

The Janvier Group's offices closed early that day due to weather, and Erica was happy that she had been able to turn in her final report to Étienne Laurent the day before. She hadn't told Josh that she was finished; she didn't want him wondering why she had finished before the gala, instead of after the gala when his final report and recommendations were due.

Erica sat in her own hotel room, using the time to prepare for penetrating Janvier's security during the gala. She decided that, since her dress was full-length, sleeveless, and strapless, she'd wear the unitard underneath and wrap its sleeves around her chest below her breasts. The balaclava and footgear, along with all of the tools she'd need, would be hidden and secured beneath the dress... and it had to be done in a way that didn't interfere with walking or dancing.

Erica had decided to wear her hair pulled back tightly into a bun, so the wind gusts wouldn't blow it out of place and so the balaclava wouldn't mess up her hair, possibly tipping off Janvier's security people that she had been wearing headgear during the party.

Inside her oversized purse, Erica had secured a pair of boots that she'd change into to make her exit. Her red overcoat was reversible and was tan on the inside. Her dress was also reversible and was black on the inside. This would allow her to enter Janvier's house in a burgundy dress and red overcoat with pumps, and walk out in a black dress and tan overcoat with boots. This was designed to make it more difficult to identify the person stealing the item from the sixth-floor gallery, should any of the security cameras be working properly during the snowstorm.

Erica went through the plans in her head over and over again. She knew the layout of Janvier's home, thanks to the renovation plans she had stolen, and she knew the security systems installed. She had several scenarios worked out in her mind for getting to the sixth floor, retrieving the item, and getting the item away from the house. The only thing she couldn't figure out was how to do all of that and leave the party with Josh. She needed him to get inside the house, but after that, he'd be a hindrance to what she needed to do.

I don't like thinking about him that way, but it's true. If I retrieve the item tonight, it means leaving him behind. Not a great start if we want to spend the rest of our lives together. I hope he'll understand. This is—was—my job, and I have to see it through so I can get out of this life and start a new one. What I do is not technically illegal, but it's a gray area. Well, it's too late to stop what's going to happen tonight. Once it's over, and I've explained things to him, I'll see how he feels and if he still loves me. Either way, tonight has to go well... for the client, for Aimee, and for me. If I get caught, because I didn't plan this right or I let myself get distracted, it won't matter if Josh still loves me or not. I won't be alive to know.

Erica continued securing her tools and thinking through potential scenarios that would help or hinder her plans.

Josh arrived at Erica's hotel thirty minutes later than he wanted because of traffic. The snow was coming down harder, and the winds made it difficult to see where you were going. Fortunately, Josh had allowed extra time to get to Erica's hotel and then get to Janvier's home.

Erica was waiting in the lobby when Josh's cab pulled up. She raced out and got inside the cab as soon as she saw him wave. "I was getting worried," she said as she snuggled next to him to get warm.

"We had to pull over a couple of times because the blowing snow made it impossible to see where we were going," Josh explained. "Hopefully, we'll have an easier time getting to Janvier's home."

It should have taken less than thirty minutes to reach Janvier's house, but it took just over an hour. Fortunately, Josh had taken this into account, and they arrived on Janvier's street close to the time that Josh wanted to arrive.

There was a long line of cars waiting to be parked and cabs dropping off quests for the gala. Josh and Erica stayed inside the cab until they reached the valet stand.

Josh paid the driver just as one of Marco's men opened the door. Erica exited the cab, followed by Josh. Josh pulled out his invitation, but the man said, "Show it to the guard at the door. Enjoy your evening."

Josh and Erica joined the queue waiting to enter Janvier's house.

"Did you see that guy?" Erica whispered.

"He looks like a walking tank," Josh joked quietly. "Janvier must be serious about security tonight."

Erica nodded. She looked around to see if Janvier had installed any new security features outside the house. She didn't see any.

When they reached the front door, Josh handed his invitation to the guard, who looked like the twin of the man at the valet stand. The guard took the invitation, examined it, and then handed it back to Josh. "Enjoy your evening. You may check your coats and bags just inside, to the right."

"Thank you," Josh said politely, noticing the bulge of a weapon under the guard's jacket.

After they checked their coats and Erica's oversized purse, Josh saw Étienne Laurent talking to Raphaël Janvier nearby. Laurent motioned for Josh to come over. Josh escorted Erica to the two men.

"Good to see you, Josh," Laurent said. "Glad you could make it here in this weather."

"I wouldn't have missed this party for any reason," Josh said.

Laurent turned to Janvier. "Raphaël, you remember Josh MacGregor, the consultant we hired to help with our expansion plans?"

Janvier smiled and nodded. "Yes, I do. Welcome to my home, Josh."

"Thank you," Josh said. He gestured to Erica. "May I introduce Erica Longwood, who is also providing consulting work to your company."

Janvier smiled broadly. "Ah, Miss Longwood. May I say how stunning you look in that dress? I've heard good things about you from Étienne. I look forward to seeing your final report. Welcome to my home. I hope you enjoy yourself this evening."

"I'm sure I will," Erica said politely.

Janvier looked at Erica and Josh. "I didn't know that the two of you were acquainted."

"We actually met on the train to Paris," Erica said. "Josh was on his way to start working for you, and I was heading to

Paris in search of new clients for my firm."

"A chance meeting, eh?" Janvier asked. "How typically Parisian. Well, please enjoy my home. There's a bar on this level and downstairs, the food is on this level, and there are sitting areas up to the fifth floor. The floors above that are closed off for the party, but please make use of any facilities on the other floors."

"Thank you," Josh and Erica both said.

The power suddenly went off.

"Damn!" Janvier cursed under his breath. "That's the fifth time since guests started arriving. If the power company wasn't so finicky, I'd switch over to the generators and shut off the city electricity, but they'll only let me switch to generators after the power has been off for two minutes or more."

The power came back on. "See? The power's never off long enough to switch to the generators. I'm glad the kitchen is gas, or the food would be ruined."

Josh and Erica nodded and stepped aside so Janvier could greet his other guests.

"By the way, our host is right," Josh whispered. "You do look stunning tonight."

"You've seen this dress before," Erica pointed out.

"I stand by my statement," Josh insisted.

Once they had moved out of the foyer, Josh and Erica headed down the central stairs to the basement to find the bar. The power dimmed as they descended the stairs, but it stayed on this time.

"That's got to play hell with the electronics around the house," Josh noted.

"And the security system," Erica added, keeping her voice steady to hide her delight. "I imagine the system will be resetting itself all night."

Josh and Erica accepted glasses of champagne from the bartender in the basement. Half of the basement was a single, large room with multiple sitting areas—decorated with Danish Modern furnishings, which Erica hated. The rest of the basement included a small home gym and a long lap pool visible through a glass wall on one side of the bar room. Most of the seats were taken, so Josh and Erica decided to explore the rest of the house.

As they walked through the house, Josh was stunned at the décor. The walls were white with gold leaf accents on the moldings and wainscoting. All of the ceilings were painted to match the sky during different seasons and weather patterns. Huge mirrors were placed on the walls to make each of the rooms appear bigger than they were, even though they were quite large without the mirrors.

The central staircase wound from the basement up to the top floor. Sconces on each of the landings provided light, as did the spotlights illuminating the paintings on the walls, the magnificent chandelier at the top, and the two stained glass skylights on either side of the chandelier.

A pianist on the second floor was playing background music as Josh and Erica headed for the dining room, where the buffet had been set up. They each filled their plates and continued exploring. The first floor was divided into a number of living rooms toward the front of the house, with the kitchen and dining room toward the rear.

The second level had several sitting areas on the west side of the central stairs, and guest rooms on the east side. The piano was on the landing, and there was a small crowd standing around the piano, listening to the music and requesting songs.

The third and fourth levels were similar to the second level, with guest rooms on the east side, but the third level had a den and the fourth level had the library on the west side.

The fifth level had what looked like an art gallery on the west side, and a home theatre on the east side. There was a circular bar on the landing. Josh and Erica refreshed their drinks at the bar and then sat on one of the benches in the gallery, admiring Janvier's art collection while they ate. The lights had dimmed or gone out three times since they entered the house.

"This is an impressive home," Josh said quietly. "You're a designer. What's your impression?"

"It's an interesting mix of styles," Erica noted after having viewed each room with the critical eye of an interior designer. "The house is designed to look old, even though it's not as old as it appears. Most of the common rooms are designed to impress, based on the use of mirrors and gold leaf. The furnishings are comfortable and more practical than I'd expect, except for the basement. I can't stand Danish Modern. The artwork is breathtaking and probably worth more than the rest of the house. And the use of materials on each floor is designed to evoke a particular mood or emotion. It was all very well done, but it's not an interior design scheme that I'd typically recommend to a client. There are too many different styles represented, and I prefer to keep the styles more consistent... and more in line with the exterior."

Erica glanced up at the ceiling. "I'd love to see what's on the sixth and seventh floors." She gestured toward the guard standing next to the velvet ropes blocking the stairs leading to those two floors. "But I don't think *he* will let anyone go up there."

"There seems to be a lot of security here tonight," Josh commented. "And those are some of the biggest guards I've ever seen." He glanced at the guard near the stairs. "And you can tell that they're well-armed. You can see the bulges under their jackets."

Erica nodded. "I counted four so far. One outside on the street, one at the front door, one in that room off the kitchen, and one here."

"I saw a fifth one," Josh added. "He was standing in the corner behind the piano on the second-floor landing."

"For a man who has security cameras everywhere, he sure

has a lot of guards present. I guess it's because of the power grid instability. All the switching between electrical power and battery back-ups is probably making the system next to useless tonight."

"It's not like he'd be worried about someone walking out with his possessions," Josh commented. "Most of which are too big and heavy to carry." He gestured toward the painting on the wall in front of them. "Could you see someone trying to carry out *that* painting?"

Erica laughed. "No. You're right. It's too big, as are the sculptures on several of the floors."

The lights dimmed twice and went out for nearly a minute. Then they came back on, flickered, and stayed on.

"It's a pity this had to happen the night of his annual party." Josh drained his glass of champagne. "I suspect Janvier is not someone who likes it when things don't go perfectly."

Erica kept a close watch on the security guard barring the way to the sixth floor. There were fewer people on the fifth floor, so she and Josh decided to stay there, dividing their time between the circular bar on the landing and the art gallery—both of which provided Erica a clear view of the guard and the stairs.

Erica noted that with each power blink, the lights stayed off longer. *I'm glad I have my night vision monocular with me. I may need it.*

Erica glanced out the window and saw that the snow was falling even harder. *The lights should start going out more frequently. After the next blink, I'll suggest that Josh meet me in the theatre while I go to the bathroom next to the bar to freshen up. There should be enough room in there for me to change and get ready to head upstairs.*

She stared at the guard, and then she looked closely at the

stairs. *I think I know how to get around that thug.*

A few minutes later, the lights began dimming as the Parisian power grid continued to be overloaded from the demand caused by the extreme weather.

"I need to hit the restroom," Erica said softly. "Why don't you see what's going on in the theatre, and I'll join you shortly."

"Why the theatre?" Josh asked.

"Because I keep seeing people going in, but I don't see them coming out. Either they're all sleeping comfortably, or there's something in there keeping their attention."

Josh nodded. "Okay. Don't be long."

"I won't."

Josh walked to the theatre, and Erica headed for the restroom. When she entered, she was pleased to see that there were three stalls. She set her champagne glass on the ledge over the sinks and walked to the far stall. She entered, closing and latching the door behind her.

She stepped out of her pumps, then unzipped and removed her dress. She pulled the unitard up and put her arms through the sleeves. She removed the drawstring bag attached by a small belt at her waist. Inside was her balaclava and her soft-soled boots. She put them on, put her pumps in the bag, and hung it and the dress on the stall door.

Her toolkit was strapped to her inner thigh. She also had an empty drawstring bag hanging from her waist, and her night vision monocular was in a pouch at her waist. She double-checked everything, and then she waited.

A few minutes later, the power dimmed again and then went out. Erica knew she had no more than two minutes before the generator kicked in or the lights turned back on. She grabbed her monocular and raced out of the restroom, grabbing the champagne glass as she ran.

When she exited the restroom, she saw that the guard had not moved. She flung her glass at the wall away from where the guard was standing. When it shattered, she saw the guard move toward the sound. She raced toward the stairs, barely making any sound at all. She leaped for the railing and vaulted over, landing on the fifth step from the bottom. She was at the top of the stairs on the sixth-floor landing in no time. Looking back, the guard was clearly unaware that anyone had passed him in the darkness.

On both the east side and the west side of the central stairs were the private art galleries. Erica went to the entrance of the east gallery and used her monocular to look for the item she was there to recover. Not seeing "The Van der Waal Peacock," she raced to the west gallery, where she not only saw "The Van der Waal Peacock," but she also saw the stolen Rembrandt, Van Gogh, Picasso, and Monet paintings.

Damn! I thought the "Charing Cross Bridge, London" had been destroyed. Erica had to remind herself that she was not there to recover the paintings. It was the peacock that she needed to retrieve.

She looked for the lasers that she knew were part of the alarm system, but the power outage and turned them off. She looked for the cameras, knowing that they were on battery backup by now, but with the monitoring station on the first floor out of power, no one could see what they were recording.

She looked at the display case holding the peacock. *The alarm is off, but as soon as the lights come back on, it'll sound. I'd better move quickly.*

She raced into the gallery and went to the display case holding the 18-inch-tall peacock. She grabbed the Plexiglas lid and shifted it. It moved. *Good. It's not attached.* She removed it and set it on the floor.

She reached for the peacock. She knew it was supposed to be heavy, but she was surprised at how heavy it was. *Thirty pounds my ass! This feels almost forty.* She grabbed the drawstring bag at her waist and carefully put the peacock inside. She pressed the outer bag in two places and broke two compressed air cylinders, which filled the outer bag with air to hold the peacock in place and prevent damage to the piece from jostling. She set the bag on the floor.

She placed her calling card on the empty pedestal and put the Plexiglas lid back on the displace case. Then she grabbed the bag and exited the gallery.

She looked down the stairs to the fifth level, but she didn't see the guard. She quickly moved down the stairs in the darkness, holding the monocular in one hand and the drawstring bag with the peacock inside in the other.

As she approached the bottom of the stairs, she saw the guard in the fifth-floor art gallery. She sat on the railing and swung her legs over the side, landing on the floor. She raced to the restroom and quietly entered. She headed for the far stall, where she had left her dress and shoes.

The lights flickered and came back on. She glanced at her watch. *Just under two minutes. Wow!*

She placed the drawstring bag with the peacock in it on the floor. She pulled off the top of the unitard, wrapped the sleeves around her chest below her breasts, and removed the balaclava and her boots. After removing her pumps and dress from the bag hanging on the stall door, she put the balaclava and boots into the bag.

She heard the alarms go off. *The alarm system has reset. That took longer than I expected.*

She removed the toolkit from her leg. After extracting a strange looking hook and a length of heavy-duty fishing line, she placed the toolkit in the bag with her balaclava. Then she put on the dress, reversing it so the black side was now facing out. She slipped on her pumps and reached up to make certain that her hair was still in place.

She attached the hook to the drawstrings of the bags holding the peacock and her balaclava and toolkit. Then she looped the fishing line through the hook. Holding the bags carefully, she exited the stall and waited.

She heard the sounds of heavy feet running up the stairs. She estimated two people were heading to the sixth floor. *The other three must be guarding all the exits.*

The lights flickered again and went out, and Erica moved quickly. She exited the restroom. Using her monocular, she confirmed that there we no guards on the fifth floor. She ran for the front windows overlooking the street, put the monocular in the bag with her toolkit and balaclava, and hung the two bags on the back of the curtain rod by the hook. Then she headed for the theatre to wait for security to start rounding up and searching the guests.

Once she was inside the theatre, she found an empty seat and waited.

I wonder if Josh is still in here or if he's out looking for me.

The lights came back on, and Erica looked around. There were a lot of people in the theatre, but she didn't see Josh. A moment later, two security guards entered the theatre, both carrying flashlights.

"There has been an incident," one of the guards stated. "We need all of you to follow us to the second floor."

Josh had been in the theatre when the lights went off. He was worried about Erica, but it was too dark to try to look for her. When the lights came back on, he didn't see her in the theatre, so he left and looked for her in the bar and art gallery. Not seeing her there, he went down to the fourth floor to see if she had gone there for some reason. The alarms sounded just before he reached the fourth-floor landing.

He bumped into Laurent in the fourth-floor library.

"What's that racket?" Josh asked.

"Security alarm," Laurent said.

"What's it for?"

"No idea," Laurent replied, "but I'm sure someone will let us know shortly." Looking at Josh, he added, "You look lost."

"Actually, Étienne, I've lost my date in all the confusion with the lights," Josh replied. "I was in the theatre waiting for her, then the lights went out, and now I can't find her."

"I'm sure she'll turn up," Laurent said. "There aren't that many places to hide in this house."

Josh smiled, but then two security guards entered the library. "Everyone follow us to the second floor," one of them said. "There has been an incident."

Laurent stood. "What's going on?"

"An object has been stolen, Mr. Laurent. From the sixth floor."

Laurent nodded.

"I didn't think we were allowed on the sixth floor," Josh said as he followed Laurent to the stairs.

"No one is allowed up there. That's why there was a guard at the foot of the stairs. That's where Raphaël's office is located. It's also where he keeps many of his prized possessions."

The second floor sitting rooms were rapidly filling up with the women when Josh and Laurent arrived. The men were directed to remain on the landing.

A few minutes later, Josh saw Erica coming down the stairs with some of the people he had seen in the theatre. *Was she there the whole time and I just missed her? Wait... is her dress black? I thought she was wearing the dark red dress she wore Christmas Eve. Maybe it's a trick of the lighting.* He waved to her and she waved back, but before they could speak, the guards hustled her into the sitting rooms with the other women.

Josh heard someone shouting from the first floor. "May I have your attention please?" He recognized the voice as Janvier's.

The crowd quieted down. "Thank you. I regret to inform

you that someone has stolen something of mine from the sixth floor. A search is underway for the item. If it is recovered, you will all be allowed to leave. If the item is not recovered, I'm afraid it will be necessary to question each of you as we try to find the culprit and the object that was stolen. I am truly sorry about this, and my men will do everything they can to minimize the inconvenience. Thank you."

Josh was worried for Erica, but he couldn't see where she was.

Erica found Janvier's reaction fascinating. *I wonder if a crook like Janvier would suspect that a woman could beat his security.*

She knew she needed to stay calm and wait until the guards had finished their search. *I hope no one looks up if they decide to search behind the curtains. All these weeks would have been wasted if they find the item while it's still in the house.*

Thirty minutes later, Janvier made another announcement. "The item has not yet been found. We'll be interviewing the women first, then the men. Once you've been interviewed, you are free to leave. Couples may wait for their significant other in the basement lounge."

The interviews were conducted in the third-floor den. There was a guard posted on the stairs leading up to the fourth floor, and all of the guards carried flashlights. Three women at a time were escorted to the third floor to be interviewed.

Erica had to wait nearly an hour before it was her turn. The lights dimmed and went out several times while she waited, but the interviews continued even while the lights were off.

When it was finally her turn, she was taken upstairs. She caught a glimpse of Josh and waved to him. He waved back.

When she was seated, one of the guards asked, "What is your name?"

"Erica Longwood."

"Who are you here with?"

"Josh MacGregor."

"What time did you arrive?"

"I have no idea. It was sometime around eight."

"How did you arrive?"

"By cab."

"Where were you when the alarm went off?"

"I was in the fifth-floor restroom next to the bar. I was heading back to the theatre to find Josh when I heard it."

"Where were you before the alarm sounded?"

"In the restroom."

"And before that?"

"In the fifth-floor art gallery with Josh."

"When you returned to the theatre, did you find Josh?"

"No," Erica replied. "I didn't see him until I was brought to the second floor. He was already there when I arrived."

"Did you go to the sixth floor?"

"No. I didn't think that was allowed. Besides, there was a guard at the foot of the stairs."

"Why were you on the fifth floor for so long?"

"It was quiet, it wasn't crowded, and it had its own bar."

"Please stand."

Erica stood. The guard produced a scanning wand, like airport security uses to find hidden objects on passengers.

"Hold your arms out."

Erica complied.

The guard used the wand to look for any metal on Erica. The only metal she had on was her earrings, her necklace, one ring on her fingers, and her watch. When the guard was finished making certain that she didn't have the peacock or any burglary tools underneath her dress, she was allowed to leave.

As she walked past the second-floor landing on her way to the basement, she waved to Josh again, who waved back.

She reached the basement, which was filling up with women waiting for their husbands and dates. *I'll bet Janvier will wish that he had interviewed couples together so they could leave sooner.*

Erica thought back to the renovation plans she had seen of the house. *There's a staircase that goes from the first floor to the seventh floor at the far end of the east side of the house. I don't think I can reach those stairs. But there's also a staircase that goes from the basement to the fifth floor, that's used by the staff to bring food and alcohol from the basement and kitchen to the bar and theatre on the fifth floor. I might be able to get up those stairs, retrieve the peacock, and get back down before the lights come back on. I just have to find where door to the stairs is hidden on this floor.*

She looked around, trying to keep from attracting the notice of anyone monitoring the security cameras. She walked slowly across the front of the bar, and next to the door leading to one of the restrooms was another door, labeled "Stairs."

The lights dimmed several times, and then they went off.

Erica kicked off her pumps, grabbed them, and raced for the door. It wasn't locked. She entered the stairway, and in the pitch black, she ran up as quickly and as quietly as she could.

When she reached the fifth floor, she sprinted across the landing to the front window and retrieved the bags she had hung on the curtain rod.

She opened the window and shuddered as a blast of cold hit her. She looked down at the front entrance and the large Tuscan Cypress Trees flanking the front porch and steps on both sides. Then she attached the fishing line to the hook on the drawstrings and lowered the bags out the windows. Just before the bags reached the Tuscan Cypress Trees, she swung the line so the bags would land on the side of the trees opposite the front porch. When the bags landed in the snow, she tossed the fishing line into the trees, closed the window, and sprinted back to the staircase at the rear of the house.

She carefully made her way downstairs to the basement. The lights blinked a couple of times, but didn't come back on until she reached the basement door. She put her pumps back on, exited the stairs, entered the restroom next door, and waited for the lights to come back on. When they did, she exited the restroom and ordered a drink from the bar.

After a while, some of the men entered the basement to find their wives and dates so they could leave the party. Erica decided it was time to join them. She followed a group upstairs, retrieved her coat and purse, and left the house.

Her overcoat was turned so that the red side was facing out. When she reached the bottom of the front steps, the power blinked again and then went out. Erica ran around to the other side of the Tuscan Cypress Trees and felt around the snow at the base of the trees until she found the bags. She removed them from the fishing line, removed the boots from her oversized purse, and put the bags in the purse.

Balancing on one leg, she took off the right pump and pulled on the right boot. Then she did the same with the left pump and boot. She reversed her overcoat so the tan side was facing out, wrapped her head and neck with her scarf, put the pumps in her purse, walked back to the front sidewalk, and joined the queue waiting for the valet and cabs. The snow was coming down so hard that any evidence of someone leaving the sidewalk, and walking to the other side of the trees and back, was obliterated in under a minute.

The lights came back on a moment later. Erica looked back at the house, but she was filled with conflicting emotions. She was elated that she had recovered the peacock, but she was about to betray Josh by leaving him with no explanation and no warning.

After I deliver the package to Aimee, I'll go back to my hotel, pack, and check out. Then I'll meet Josh at his hotel and explain everything to him.

She reached the front of the line for cabs and was soon heading for the rendezvous with Aimee.

CHAPTER 10

Josh waited for his turn to be interrogated. He was asked the same questions that Erica had been asked, but the guards seemed particularly interested by the fact that he and Erica got separated right before the alarms went off. After he was scanned with the wand, he was allowed to leave.

He raced down to the basement, but Erica was not there. Confused and worried, he sent her a text: *"I'm in the basement looking for you. Where are you?"*

There was no response.

He texted her again.

No response.

He tried to call, but it went straight to voicemail.

He headed up to the first floor to see if her overcoat and purse were there. When he discovered they were gone, he was even more confused. *Why did she leave? Maybe she wasn't feeling well. I should head over to her hotel and see if she's all right.*

He grabbed his coat and left the house to catch a cab to Erica's hotel.

Erica's cab arrived at the rendezvous with Aimee. "Wait for me," she said to the driver.

"Okay."

She walked over to Aimee's car. Aimee rolled down the window, and Erica handed her the bag containing "The Van der Waal Peacock."

Aimee peeked inside the bag and smiled. "Fantastic work, Erica. I'm proud of you. You came through for us, and the client will be pleased."

"Janvier has a lot of stolen art on the sixth floor of his house," Erica said. "I saw Rembrandt's 'The Storm on the Sea of Galilee,' Van Gogh's 'Poppy Flowers,' Picasso's 'Le Pigeon aux Petits Pois,' and Monet's 'Charing Cross Bridge, London' in the west gallery where the peacock was on display."

Aimee snorted. "Impossible. 'Charing Cross Bridge, London' was destroyed by the thieves who stole it. Everyone knows that."

"And yet it's hanging on the wall next to the Picasso," Erica insisted.

"So what?"

"Don't you think the authorities would be interested in knowing that Janvier is in possession of millions of euros worth of stolen art?"

"And how would we explain how we knew about it?" Aimee demanded.

Erica stared at her. "Aimee, our client for the peacock is an insurance company. Insurance companies have relationships with Interpol. You tell our client, who already knows how we know that the art is there. They tell Interpol, Janvier gets arrested, and no one besides our client has any idea that we were involved."

Aimee held Erica's gaze. "Fine. I'll let them know."

"Thank you. And don't forget to wire my half of the recovery fee."

"And what about your expenses?"

"The contract with Janvier more than covered those."

Aimee nodded. Then she asked, "Are you sure you won't change your mind about leaving?"

"I'm sure. It's been a good run, but it's time for me to bow out and let someone else do the breaking and entering work. I'm tired, and I'm ready for a change."

"I'll miss you," Aimee said.

"I'll miss you, too. You're my oldest friend. Maybe we can get together or talk from time to time... as long as we don't talk about work."

Aimee laughed. "I might just take you up on that."

Erica leaned in and gave Aimee a hug. "Take care of yourself."

"You, too, Erica. You, too."

Aimee drove off, and Erica headed back to her cab. As she drove to her hotel, Erica thought, *I always thought it would be hard to walk away, but it was actually the easiest thing I've ever done. Now, I just need to repair a bridge with Josh, and we can start living new lives on our own terms.*

Josh arrived at the Hotel Elysées Ceramic after midnight. He went up to Erica's room and knocked on the door.

Erica opened the door, and her eyes opened wide when she saw Josh standing there. She hugged him and pulled him inside her room. "Oh, my god, you're here. What happened to you?"

"What happened to me?" Josh asked, "What happened to you? I texted and called, but you didn't answer. Why didn't you wait for me?"

"My phone died," Erica said. "And I was feeling nauseated. I thought about going to your hotel, but mine was closer, and the roads were terrible."

Josh looked around and saw Erica's suitcases on her bed.

Next to it was her dress, which he saw was black on the outside and dark red on the inside "You're packing? What's going on?"

"I was going to come over to your hotel, since we're only in Paris until the end of the week," she answered. "With all the snow, I didn't want us to get stuck in different parts of the city with no way to see each other."

Josh stared into her eyes. Then he pointed to the dress. "There's something you're not telling me. There's more going on here, and I want to know what it is. Why did you arrive in a red dress and leave in a black dress? What happened to you tonight? You disappeared before the lights went off, then the alarms went off, and then you left Janvier's home without me. What were you doing when we were separated?"

"I already told you—"

"I want the truth this time."

Erica froze. Then she said, "This was a conversation I was going to have with you in Antigua. Wouldn't you rather wait until we get there?"

Josh shook his head. He sat in one of the chairs near the bed and gestured for her to sit on the bed across from him.

"Where do you want me to start," Erica asked.

"What happened tonight?"

Erica looked very uncomfortable. "You can't breathe a word of this to anyone, understood?"

Josh nodded.

"Janvier is a crook. Oh, The Janvier Group is a legitimate business... mostly. But the bulk of his empire is illegal. In addition to being a smuggler and a trafficker, he collects art."

"We saw that tonight."

Erica shook her head. "No, you saw what was on the fifth floor. That's the art he obtained legally. On the sixth floor, he has two art galleries, and that's the art he had stolen for him. He has millions upon millions in stolen art on that floor."

"Why does that matter to you?"

"Because I'm an art recovery specialist," Erica admitted.

"What?! I thought you were an interior designer."

"I'm that, too. And a good one. But it's mostly a front for my real job. I recover stolen artwork and return it to the proper owner."

"You're a thief? Like... some kind of cat burglar?" Josh leaned forward with his head between his hands. "I'm in love with a thief?"

"I'm not a thief," Erica protested. "People like Janvier are the thieves. We're hired by the rightful owners and insurance companies to retrieve stolen items. We don't keep or sell what we recover. If we did, then we *would* be thieves."

"So, you steal art back, and you give it back to the owners?"

Erica nodded. "Yes!"

"So, what did Janvier steal that you stole back?"

"'The Van der Waal Peacock.' It's a solid gold, jewel encrusted eighteen-inch-tall peacock created by Horst Van der Waal that was insured for thirty million euros by the man who commissioned the piece for his wife. Janvier had it stolen, and the insurance company contacted us to recover it."

"I assume you get paid for your work."

Erica shrugged. "Insurance companies pay us ten percent of the insured value for a recovery, and I get half of that. Sometimes we work for the individuals who were robbed, and the rate is usually the same. Sometimes we work *pro bono* for clients who can't afford our fees. I had one of those clients in Barcelona right before I met you."

Josh did the math. "So, you got paid one-and-a-half million for stealing this peacock back from Janvier?"

Erica nodded.

Josh shook his head. Then he sat up. "Wait a minute. Did you use me to gain access to Janvier?"

Erica's head dropped, and her face turned red. She looked

at Josh with a guilty expression on her face. "At first." When Josh turned angry, she added, "But just at first. I was attracted to you immediately. Then I thought you might be able to help me get to Janvier, so I reached out to you, but the more we spent time together, the deeper in love I fell. I wanted to come clean with you. I wanted to tell you everything. But I knew I had to wait until I had recovered the peacock. It was too dangerous to tell you the truth, particularly with Janvier's reputation of killing anyone who crosses him. My life was at risk; your life would have been at risk, too. I had to make sure you were protected, so I said nothing. But everything I felt, everything I said to you, everything we did together, all that was real—from the heart. It wasn't just to help me get the job done."

"How can I believe that?" Josh demanded. "I got you the job at The Janvier Group, and I got you into Janvier's house tonight. You made me think it was my idea all along, but it wasn't, was it? It was you pulling the strings so you could get your job done, and to hell with me and my feelings."

"That's not true! Damnit, Josh, I quit my job. Tonight was my last recovery. I've left that life for good so I can start a new one with you. I love you, and I've never loved anyone before. Not really. My God, do you actually think I'd sleep with you just to get a job done? I'd never do that! I don't sleep with targets, and I don't sleep with people to get them to give me access to targets. I'm not a whore."

Josh stood. "I don't know what to think. I don't know what to believe anymore. I've fallen in love with you, I've decided to walk away from my career for you, and now I find out that it all started with a lie because I was a means to an end for you. I can't... I don't... How am I supposed to trust you?"

Tears poured down Erica's face. "Because you know in your heart that I love you and that everything we shared was real. Everything!"

Josh turned his back on her. "I need time to think. I need to process this."

"Will you come with me to Antigua?" Erica pleaded.

Josh shook his head. "I need time to... I... I can't think straight right now. I have to go."

"I'm leaving for Antigua as soon as flights resume at the airport," Erica said as she followed him to the door. "If you join me, then I'll know you realized that I truly, deeply, completely love you. If not, then I'll know it was all just a fantasy that you decided to end... for both of us."

Josh shot her an angry look, and then he left without a word. Erica closed the door and sank to the floor, crying uncontrollably.

The next day, The Janvier Group was still closed due to weather. Josh spent the day in his hotel room, finishing his report and recommendations to The Janvier Group. It was all he could think of to do to get Erica off his mind.

He didn't have a problem with the fact that she recovered stolen art. His problem is that she used him to get to Janvier. *I was just a mark for her con game. How am I supposed to trust her? How do I believe a thing that she says?*

On Thursday morning, the snow had stopped and the roads were clear, making it possible for Josh to return to his office at The Janvier Group. When he left his hotel room to take the shuttle to The Carpe Diem building, there was an envelope waiting for him under the door. He put it in his briefcase and headed for the office.

When he arrived, Étienne Laurent stuck his head in the door. "How are you this morning?"

"Still a little shaken up," Josh admitted.

"I understand. I've never experienced anything like that before."

"Did the item get recovered?" Josh asked.

Laurent shook his head. "How did Erica handle what happened?"

Josh shrugged. "You know women. They're resilient about some things and... not so resilient about others. She seemed... okay when I talked to her after the party." Josh felt guilty about Erica leaving her project unfinished. *I should apologize to Étienne for recommending Erica to him.*

Laurent interrupted Josh's thoughts, "When you see her again, give her my thanks for her final designs. It's one of the most thorough space utilization, migration, and redesign plans I've ever seen. She provided recommendations for every bit of office space we have in northern France, contracts with new landlords that will save us millions each year, plus buildout designs and interior designs for the space that include furniture, fabrics, color schemes, artwork, and security. I've never seen anything like it before. I wanted to hire her to oversee the implementation, but she recommended three companies to handle that for us—a renovation contractor, a security company, and an interior design firm. Raphaël has worked with these companies before, so he's onboard with her recommendations. Please, tell her from all of us that she did an outstanding job and we couldn't be more pleased."

Josh tried to hide his surprise. "I will. Thank you."

Laurent left, and Josh sat there with his mind reeling. *She actually finished her project? It wasn't all just a ruse? Did I misjudge her?*

Josh emailed his final report and recommendations to Laurent and to Peter Olivetti in London. Then Josh started making his travel plans, since the next day—Friday—was his last day with The Janvier Group. It would also be his last day with his consulting firm, although he hadn't told his boss yet.

He started searching for flights out of Paris, and then he remembered the envelope he found under his hotel room door

162

that morning. He pulled it out and opened it.

Inside was an itinerary for a reservation in his name from Paris to London, and then from London to Antigua. There was also a handwritten note.

Dear Josh,

I love you. I never planned on falling for you, but love is never planned; it just happens. I will do whatever it takes to earn your trust so we can be together. Yes, I have recovered stolen artwork for my clients, but you have stolen my heart. I have changed my ways and walked away from that life, and I'll do anything else you ask so we can be together. If you get off the plane in Antigua, it'll make me the happiest person in the world. If you don't, I'll understand. Either way, I'll have my answer.

All my love, Erica (AKA Le Chat Rusé)

P.S. You should probably know that Erica Longwood isn't my real name. My real name is Erica Culpepper. Everything else I told you about myself is true. When I started working in Europe, I changed my last name to protect my parents.

Josh stared at the note and the itinerary. Then he put them back into the envelope and put the envelope back into his briefcase. He opened the travel agency app on his laptop and began searching for flights to Atlanta, Georgia.

The next morning, Josh's boss called him from London.

"Congratulations, Josh," Peter Olivetti, Senior Partner with EPDHW Consulting LLP, said when Josh answered. "I just got off the phone with Étienne Laurent at The Janvier Group, and we've been awarded the implementation contract for your recommendations! It's all thanks to you. Oh, and welcome aboard, Partner."

"Partner?"

"Yes, Partner. Remember when I told you that if you sold the implementation of your recommendations, the other partners would vote you in? Well, you did, and they did. Now, you'll need to come to London as soon as possible for the promotion ceremony, and we'll need to assemble a team to send to Paris to replace you. Then you'll need to meet with sales and marketing to start identifying opportunities in your territories. After that—"

"I need to stop you there, Peter," Josh interrupted. "I'm not accepting the promotion."

"What?!"

"No. In fact, today is my last day with the firm. I'm getting out while I'm still young enough to enjoy what life has to offer."

"What are you talking about?" Peter demanded. "You're being awarded a partnership in the premier consulting firm in Europe. This is the big leagues. This is big money. How can you just walk away from that?"

"How many times have you been divorced, Peter?" Josh asked.

"Twice... going on a third," Peter replied. "Why?"

"And apart from alimony and child support, what do you spend your money on?"

"I don't understand the question. I have a great flat in London, I have a super expensive sports car..."

"Yes, but when was the last time you took a vacation that wasn't also a business trip?"

"Oh, well... I... wait, there was... no... I... I can't remember."

"And that's my point. I have a ton of money in the bank that I don't spend. I live in hotels, I eat room service, and I'll probably die alone with all that money still in the bank, doing nothing for no one... unless I get out now and live the life that I should have been living all along. I don't want to be divorced. I don't want to be alone. I don't want to measure my life's worth in terms of my work. I don't want my headstone to read, 'Here lies a hard worker who died alone, unloved, and uncelebrated.' I see the path that you want me to take, and I'm rejecting it. I'm sorry, Peter, but I resign… effective immediately."

There was a pause on the line. Then Peter said, "Look, Josh, if you need time to see a shrink about this, we'll give you a week so you can visit one of those immersive clinics. The company will pick up the tab. Go there, get your head back on straight, and then come back to work where you belong."

"No, Peter. I quit. That's it. I'm flying home to the States this weekend, and if you're smart, you'll quit and do the same. Oh, and something you should know. Janvier's a crook, and his illegal businesses have infiltrated The Janvier Group. You might want to walk away from the implementation contract. Whoever gets assigned could get their hands dirty, or they could get disappeared by Janvier's goons. Something to think about."

"I don't understand…"

"Good bye, Peter." Josh ended the call and shook his head in disbelief. *I've known people obsessed with their jobs before, but he is living proof of why I needed to quit.*

Josh took all of the company reports and documents in his office to the recycle room at the far end of the floor. Then he stopped by Laurent's office.

"I'm leaving now, Étienne," Josh said. "I wanted to thank you for the opportunity and to say good bye."

Laurent nodded. "Yes, I guess now that you're a partner, you'll be flying all over Europe instead of running client projects. Well, your last client project was a great success, and we thank you for your efforts on our behalf."

"Thank you, Étienne, but I didn't accept the partnership. I'm heading home instead."

"Home? Where's home?"

"Georgia, in the States."

"You're returning to America? Well, I hope you're as successful there as you were here."

Josh just smiled. "Thank you. And thank Raphaël when you see him. I appreciate everything."

Laurent's phone rang. He waved to Josh as he answered the call.

Josh grabbed his briefcase and overcoat. He returned his badges to Security, and then he left The Carpe Diem building for the last time. As he rode the shuttle back to his hotel, he wondered how he'd look back on his time in Paris. *Will this be remembered as the city of love, or just my last consulting assignment?*

Sunday morning, Josh sat in one of the departure lounges at Paris Charles de Gaulle/Roissy Airport. His Delta business class flight to Atlanta was scheduled to depart at ten minutes after two o'clock that afternoon. He had just finished reading the front-page newspaper article about Interpol's raid on Janvier's house and the recovery of almost a billion euros in stolen artwork. *Is Erica behind this? Did she tip off Interpol? I wonder if Peter saw the article. I wonder if it will induce him to drop Janvier as a client.* As he tossed the paper into the trash, he looked around and was struck by the complete absence of holiday decorations inside the airport. It looked like just another day.

The thought of decorations made him think of Erica, despite how hard he tried not to. The time they had spent over the Christmas holidays were some of the happiest days and happiest memories of his life, and in that moment, those memories and feelings came flooding into his mind.

Why can't I forget her and just move on? Why do I feel like a part of me—the best part of me—is missing because she's not here? Everything feels empty. I feel empty.

He shook his head in frustration. A moment later, he heard an announcement over the intercom.

"Attention please. Virgin Atlantic announces that their flight to London begins boarding in ten minutes. All confirmed passengers should make their way to the gate immediately."

Josh thought there was something familiar about a ten o'clock Virgin Atlantic flight to London. Then he remembered the itinerary that was left under his hotel room door. He reached into his briefcase and took out the envelope. It showed that he had a reservation on that flight, with a two-hour-and-ten-minute layover at Heathrow Airport, followed by a nine-hour flight to Antigua that arrived at five-fifty-five local time.

He stared at the itinerary, and then he re-read the note from Erica. *I still love her. I may not like how and why things started between us, but I love where they went. I know my feelings were real, and if she wants me to join her in Antigua, her feelings must have been real, too.*

His mind filled with his memories of her. He looked at the itinerary again, and then he made his decision. He grabbed his briefcase, and his two carry-on bags, and headed for the Delta counter. He handed his itinerary for his Atlanta flights to the Delta employee. "I need to cancel this reservation."

The Delta employee nodded. After a couple of minutes, she handed Josh the cancellation confirmation. Josh thanked her, and then he grabbed his bags and headed for the Virgin Atlantic departure gate.

Just before six o'clock local time that evening, Erica waited outside passport control at Antigua's V.C. Bird International Airport. She was nervous. She hadn't heard anything from Josh since he left her hotel room on Tuesday night. Now, it was

Sunday, and she had no idea if he was coming or if she had wasted the cost of an airline ticket.

She had shed her boots, overcoats, unitards, and other cold-weather gear. She was dressed in sandals, a floral print blouse tied high in the front, a short wrap-around skirt that showed off her legs, and a bikini underneath. But she'd trade all the sun, breezes, and warmth in the world to be with Josh again.

Will he get off that airplane?

Is he even on that airplane?

She heard the announcement that the flight from London was on the ground and would be arriving at the gate soon.

She tried to remain calm, but the longer she had to wait, the more anxious she became.

Why am I so nervous? It's only the rest of my life at stake.

After waiting nearly twenty minutes, she saw the London passengers approaching passport control and immigration with their retrieved luggage. A few minutes later, these passengers began exiting passport control, heading for the taxi queues and resort shuttles.

Erica scanned the faces, looking for the one face she longed to see. *Where is he?*

She saw fewer passengers exiting, and her heart nearly broke. She wanted to cry, but she had no tears left to shed. She decided to wait another couple of minutes before heading back to her hotel to figure out her next steps.

She thought she recognized a face, but she didn't want to get her hopes up. Still, it looked like him. He came closer, and she saw that familiar smile. It was Josh!

She ran up to him and threw her arms around him so forcefully that it nearly knocked him over.

"I just got here, Erica. Don't kill me yet."

She kissed him repeatedly. "I missed you, Josh. When you didn't call, I feared the worst. But you're here! You're really here!"

"I'm here." He kissed her back, and in the moment, he felt like he was floating again.

"Do you forgive me?" Erica asked, her eyes pleading.

"Yes, I do, as long as you promise to be completely honest with me from now on, okay? I love you with all my heart, and I want today to be the first day of our new, long life together."

"I love you, too, with all my heart." She looked around and said, "Let's get out of here and start living that new life."

The End

ABOUT THE AUTHOR

Award-winning author and publisher William Speir was born in 1962 in Birmingham, Alabama. He attended the University of Alabama, and graduated from the University of Alabama at Birmingham in 1984. He spent over 25 years in corporate America, serving as a management consultant, leader, IT executive, and HR/Payroll executive for top-tier consulting firms and Fortune 100 companies.

During William's corporate career, he published several articles on leadership and the human impact of organizational changes and technology changes.

His first experience with book publishing was with a series of ten textbooks he authored about field artillery in the 19th century. These textbooks were later consolidated into a single volume and re-published in 2015 as *Muzzle-Loading Artillery for Reenactors*.

In addition to his artillery manual, William has published 21 novels, including a 9-book action-adventure series (*The Knights of the Saltire Series*), five historical novels (*King's Ransom, The Saga of Asbjorn Thorleikson, Nicaea – The Rise of the Imperial Church, Arthur, King,* and *The Besieged Pharaoh*), one fantasy novel (*The Kingstone of Airmid*), one science fiction novel (*The Olympium of Bacchus 12*), two stand-alone action novels (*Shiko Unleashed* and *The Day of the Dead*), and two espionage/geo-political thrillers (*The Trinity Gambit* and *Codename: Mountbatten*). *Love's Second Chance* and *Stealing Love* are William's first Adult Fiction/Contemporary Romance Novels.

William is a 5-time Royal Palm Literary Award winner: 2014 Second Place Unpublished Historical Fiction for *King's Ransom*, 2015 Second Place Unpublished Historical Fiction for *The Saga of Asbjorn Thorleikson*, 2017 Second Place Published Historical Fiction for *Arthur, King*, 2017 First Place Published Historical Fiction for *Nicaea – The Rise of the Imperial Church*, and 2017 First Place Published Science Fiction for *The Olympium of Bacchus 12*.

For more information about William Speir, please visit his website at WilliamSpeir.com.

Progressive Rising Phoenix Press is an independent publisher. We offer wholesale pricing and multiple binding options with no minimum purchases for schools, libraries, book clubs, and retail vendors. We offer substantial discounts on bulk orders and discounts on individual sales through our online store. Please visit our website at:

www.ProgressiveRisingPhoenix.com

If you enjoyed reading this book, please review it on Amazon, B & N, or Goodreads. Thank you in advance!